In Fairyland

In Fairyland: The World of Tessa Farmer
Edited by Catriona McAra

ISBN: 978-1-907222-37-5

A CIP catalogue record for this book is available from the British Library.

Strange Attractor Press
BM SAP, London, WC1N 3XX, UK
www.strangeattractor.co.uk

Printed and bound by TJ International Ltd, Padstow, Cornwall.

In Fairyland:
The World of
Tessa Farmer

edited by Catriona McAra

Table of Contents

The Malevolent Nostalgia of Tessa Farmer

Catriona McAra

The first time I saw one of Tessa Farmer's sculptures
dangling discreetly in a window at Port Eliot,
I fell in love.
— *Viktor Wynd, 2011*

De-installing an exhibition of work by London-based sculptor and animator, Tessa Farmer (b.1978), is a curious process for even the most intrepid curator. It requires weaponry (scissors, tweezers, specimen jars, assortment containers), defiance in the face of gravity (a step-ladder), and a very steady hand. Vast swarms of wasps and bees are confronted, teased apart and nestled into separate compartments; antique taxidermy is cut down, wrapped and boxed, all as if this were the natural order of things. But suddenly, an anomaly rears its head! What is to be done historically, thematically, taxonomically with the winged humanoid with a crab-claw appendage? This is the moment of realisation — we are dealing with an entirely different register of reality, for the world of Tessa Farmer has lured us into fairyland.

Tessa's collection of Sylvanian Families.

Many recall their first encounter with Farmer's skeletal fairies and taxidermy specimens as an earth-shattering moment. Once her notorious beings are discovered, an engrossing fascination quickly takes over, and the viewer becomes a willing victim of her/his own curiosity. Farmer's figurative dioramas are bewitching and send us rushing back to childhood. The first time I saw Farmer's work I became enchanted.[1] In researching her work over a period of many years, all the horror stories and fantasy films that seduced and terrified me as a child have been re-animated before my eyes: the scar-faced rabbits of *Watership Down* (1978); the mice-children of *The Nutcracker Fantasy* (1979); the lab-rats in *The Secret of NIMH* (1982). I designate this feeling, this jolt of surprise coupled with a sense of *schadenfreude*, as a malevolent nostalgia.[2] That irrepressible longing I experience in the remembrance of watching such strange animations is rendered more comprehensible when looking at Farmer's fantastic evolutions. Indeed, the magical practice of Tessa Farmer has always been firmly rooted in her childhood of the 1980s, which I also recognise as my own. The miniature domains of childhood toys provided the essential foundations for her interest in play on a tiny scale. These are historically specific to the 1980s' capitalist-inspired collecting phenomena which included Sylvanian Families, Polly Pocket, Lego, and My Little Pony, though such obsessions and indoctrinations are perhaps ongoing.

Farmer's work reaches back further, and is intertextual in its spider's web of source texts. As Gail-Nina Anderson explains further, a range of Victorian and Edwardian fairy tales has been plundered by Farmer — especially the picture-book illustrations of Richard Doyle, Arthur Rackham and Beatrix Potter — as has the contemporary fairy scholarship of Marina Warner and Carole G. Silver, among numerous others. *The Flower Fairies* by Cicely Mary Barker (1923) provided Farmer with another important reference point — illustrations of child-fairies costumed and frolicking within a floral wonderland. However, Farmer's fairies are a deliberate subversion of the stereotypical pink, perky Tinkerbells of the popular imagination. Dainty but deadly, her practice offers a femininity that is not afraid of getting its hands dirty. Another well-known example of the intersection (or, indeed, confusion) between children and fairies is that of the Cottingley photographs,[3] and the notion of the 'real-fake' is everywhere apparent in Farmer's practice. Often the boundaries between who is doing the making, Farmer or her fairies, is deliberately distorted. In order to practice, Farmer has to actively believe in her fairies.

The world of Tessa Farmer bristles with myth-making, and it would seem that the art of Faerie (see Jeremy Harte) is very much in her blood. One of the most noteworthy facts about the artist is that she embarked on her fairy sculptures *before* learning that she was a descendent of the fairy-fiction and horror writer, Arthur Machen. In this volume, Machen is positioned as the lifeblood and heritage of Farmer's practice. Two of the opening contributions, by performance artist, Brian Catling, and Gothic scholar, John Sears, dwell on this peculiar coincidence. Within such a 'supernatural' gene pool, it is worth noting that such a legacy has skipped two generations:

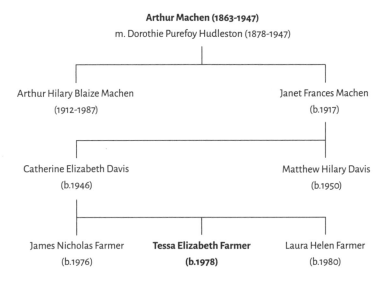

Arthur Machen (1863-1947)
m. Dorothie Purefoy Hudleston (1878-1947)

Arthur Hilary Blaize Machen (1912-1987) — Janet Frances Machen (b.1917)

Catherine Elizabeth Davis (b.1946) — Matthew Hilary Davis (b.1950)

James Nicholas Farmer (b.1976) — **Tessa Elizabeth Farmer (b.1978)** — Laura Helen Farmer (b.1980)

Ever since the first appearance of Farmer's fairies — a Thumbelina-like emergence from within a red flower in her mother's garden (c.1999) — they have been 'evolving'.[4] At The Ruskin School of Art, Farmer was made to life-draw from bones and anatomical specimens which led to her interests in the articulation of skeletal bodies. In a recent interview with Petra Lange-Berndt, Farmer explained that she constructs the fairies out of a plant root 'specifically a fern called bird's nest fern, the Latin name is *Asplenium nidus*.'[5] These roots are then secured with superglue, and the tiny fairy figure is hung with magician's thread. As Farmer elaborates in a recent television interview, insects will dry out naturally but can become quite brittle — so entomologists use a process called 'relaxing' in which a little moisture is reinfused allowing the dried-out insects to become more malleable.[6] The majority of animals in Farmer's works to date have been the woodland creatures and inhabitants of the English hedgerow (fox, mice, moles, squirrels, small birds, etc.) which are frozen then professionally stuffed. The insects that feature in her work are not always native but are often sourced from South America and Africa by expedition and mail-order. They may also be collected along the banks of her local canal in Tottenham, London, and occasionally, she even acquires treasures from the ocean such as crustaceans, urchins, barnacles, etc.

A pivotal moment in Farmer's artistic incubation was, no doubt, her Parabola residency (2007) at the Natural History Museum, London, where she became interested in a particular species of microscopic wasp known as 'fairy flies' — likely competitors for her own fluttering brood.[7] Entomology curator, Gavin R. Broad, explores Farmer's interest in the insect-world further in his contribution to this volume, particularly the seeming brutality of parasitic wasps that lay their eggs in host organisms. For a long time after her residency, a commitment to decreasing the size of her fairies became the priority. However, in early 2015, Farmer explained to me that this particular self-challenge had ceased to motivate her; the fairies could only become so minute before they disappeared from naked sight altogether! Instead it appears that she has begun to devote her creative energies to exploring their increasingly complex cornucopia of habitats. Farmer's fairies infest abandoned skulls, mount their own trophies, and, like the Borrowers, utilise dollhouse crockery for the purpose of gustation. In explaining the importance of scale, Susan Stewart reminds us that: '[t]he miniature has the capacity to make its context remarkable [...] Thistledown becomes mattress; acorn cup becomes cradle...'[8] In this way, Farmer's artmaking explicitly mimics the fairy architecture described in Michael Drayton's seventeenth century poem 'Nymphidia' (1627). With all this building of houses, and even vehicles, one would be forgiven for thinking Farmer was conjuring a new civilisation, yet the barbaric acts of her fairies resemble humanity more than we might care to acknowledge.

In addition to a series of *Flying Skull Ships*, the fairies have also 'travelled' into outer space — a perfectly logical development when one contemplates their insatiable desire for world domination. The appropriation of a dog skull, with a collar reading 'Laika' — the first dog in space — makes this all the more factually accurate (Fig 1: see colour insert). Here, space archaeology becomes a likely pursuit as the fairies colonise the floating debris that orbits around planet Earth.

Turning to a different dimension of Farmer's epistemological endeavour, Victorian pseudo-art formats (such as taxidermy specimens, butterfly pressings, and dried flowers preserved and displayed within glass bells) are very much the kernel of her practice. Developing the concerns of such late twentieth century artists as Mark Dion, Damien Hirst, and Mat Collishaw (Fig 2: see colour insert), Farmer is one facet of a lively generation of early twenty-first century creative practitioners who appropriate animal materials for the purposes of their work: Polly Morgan, Claire Morgan, Kate MccGwire, Kelly McCallum, Charles Avery, and Samantha Sweeting, among others. This taxidermy revival has, in turn, been championed by numerous collectors and scholars including Alexis Turner and Lange-Berndt.[9]

Farmer's work is perhaps unique for its inclusion of the fairy figure, which renders her work of interest to fantasy conventions as well as art historical and museological discourses. She also researches older European traditions of anatomy drawing, vanitas imagery, and curiosity cabinets — legacies which had already re-emerged in mid-twentieth century surrealism.[10] The archetypal praying mantis loomed large in the dissident surrealist imagination of Roger Caillois, while a pickled armadillo foetus appears in a ubiquitous photograph by Dora Maar (1936). The box assemblages of Joseph Cornell (Fig 3: see colour insert) also serve as nostalgic precursors of the work of Tessa Farmer, both in terms of the practice of collecting and the infatuation with the miniature.

Farmer's malevolent nostalgia is thus anachronistic as well as postmodern, what Steve Baker might refer to as a 'botched taxidermy'.[11] Some viewers find the use of dead carcasses and insects as exhibits repulsive and/or ethically challenging. Philipp Blom reminds us that to 'collect we have to kill', be it 'literally' in the act of pinning or 'metaphorically' in terms of decontextualisation.[12] Farmer, meanwhile, justifies the use of such materials in the tradition of the found object which, for her, tend to include antique taxidermy, excavated mummifications, road kill, and insects collected after dying from natural causes. Farmer is a vegetarian, acutely aware of animal rights, and her work could be said to participate in raising awareness of ecological issues. She also rescues moth-eaten, broken, museum specimens which would otherwise be facing decommission.

Returning to the crab-claw anomaly with which I began, Tessa Farmer's fairies could be said to 'undo formal categories' as in the tradition of Georges Bataille,[13] a connection explored further by Giovanni Aloi in the final chapter of this book. In total, *In Fairyland* aims to capture the multi-faceted nature of Farmer's practice. Editorially, I have resisted the temptation to divide the essays dialectically into the rigour of entomology versus the creativity of folk tales, or, more broadly, the misleading distinction of science versus art. The way I see it, the two are conjoined in the very corporeality of Farmer's fairies; one cannot exist without the other.[14] Moving beyond the scientific/ fantastic binary enables us to explore Farmer's work more accurately in terms of its infinite variety. This fantastic evolution, therefore, begins with an alternative origin of species, followed by a section more closely focused on the insidious behaviour of Farmer's fairies. Enter the domain of the enchanted entomologist! *In Fairyland* invites you on a magical journey into the malevolent world of Tessa Farmer.

Notes

1. Charlotte Sinclair, 'Small is Beautiful', *Vogue* (September 2006), 135–136.

2. This idea is inspired by Kate Bernheimer in 'This Rapturous Form', *Marvels and Tales: A Journal of Fairy-Tale Studies*, 20:1 (2006): 67–83.

3. The five Cottingley fairy photographs (1917–1920) by Elsie Wright and her cousin, Frances Griffiths, recently provided the conceptual background for a research-exhibition I curated at Leeds College of Art, *Tessa Farmer: In Fairyland with Su Blackwell, Sverre Malling and Annelies Strba* (30 January–26 February 2015). See also Marie Irving and Alistair Robinson, 'Entirely Plausible Hybrids of Humans and Insects', *Antennae: The Journal of Nature in Visual Culture*, 3:1 (2007): 13-15.

4. Louise Stern has recently described this phenomenon as Farmer's 'personally devised science', 'The Devious Fairies of Tessa Farmer', *Flotsam Fantastique: The Souvenir Book of World Fantasy Convention 2013*, edited by Stephen Jones (Brighton: PS Publishing, 2013), 117.

5. Petra Lange-Berndt, 'Small Things, Dead Things, Stingy Things: An Interview with Tessa Farmer', *Preserved!* (November 2013): http://www.preservedproject.

co.uk/small-things-dead-things-stingy-things-an-interview-with-tessa-farmer/
Accessed 20 September 2015.

6. Tessa Farmer interviewed by *Made in Leeds* (January 2015): https://vimeo.
com/127047204 Accessed 20 September 2015.

7. This residency at the Natural History Museum was brokered by curators, Bergit
Arends and Danielle Arnaud.

8. Susan Stewart, *On Longing: Narratives of the Miniature, the Gigantic, the Souvenir, the
Collection* (Durham: Duke University Press, 1993), 46.

9. See for example Alexis Turner, *Taxidermy* (London: Thames and Hudson, 2013), 27.

10. Highly recommended on this topic is the work of Marion Endt-Jones.

11. Steve Baker, *The Postmodern Animal* (London: Reaktion Books Ltd., 2000), 74.

12. Philipp Blom, *To Have and to Hold: An Intimate History of Collectors and Collecting*
(New York and Woodstock: The Overlook Press, 2002), 152.

13. Rosalind Krauss, *L'Amour Fou* (London: Hayward, 1986), 64–65.

14. See Christopher Wood, *Fairies in Victorian Art* (Suffolk: ACC Art Books, 1999), 11.

Part I
Another Origin
of Species

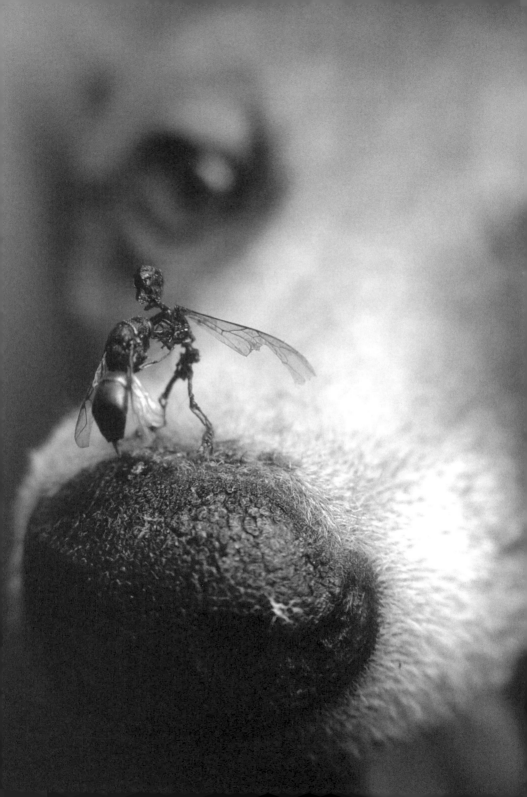

Show and Tell

Brian Catling

Ten years ago, or maybe more, an MA student quietly placed three books on the library table for our inspection and comment. This was a 'Show and Tell' session, one of the highlights of the small MA course that we ran at The Ruskin School of Drawing and Fine Art.

With only three or four graduate students each year, joint tutorial classes were prescribed in their intimacy. Malcolm Bull, my only other colleague in this venture, invented these little gatherings in which we may discover something interesting, and hopefully valuable, about each other's practice, research and obsessions. One of Bull's great pedagogic talents is his ability to unhook and remove himself from his own classified research and his international reputation as a scholastic genji of profoundly original concepts and points of view. It is rare that such erudite thinkers want to, or are capable of, achieving this generous detachment, and willingly become totally engaged in the imagination and structural thinking of others.

I am afraid I can't remember the other objects and ideas that were exposed that day. The three books and their lineage that sat so innocently in the weak filtered sunlight of an unexceptional morning have bleached out everything else. While waiting for all to arrive and settle, I casually examined them. Then I awoke; the identity of the first book jarring the moment alive. The second threw me into a confused reverie of privilege and potential treasure trove. The third left me silent. The session was beginning around me. The student who brought the books was back in the room.

'Where did you get these?'

I already knew the talented, young woman from her three previous years at The Ruskin and the distinctly original undergraduate work that she made then. I knew of her self-containment and seriousness and how lonely that can make somebody in Oxford, and how intensity can be debased as shyness on the other side of constant, imposed frivolity.

'My great-grandfather', she answered.

In my over-excited condition I misunderstood what she had just said.

'Your grandfather was a man of great taste and decision.'

I think I said, or should have, but it could equally have been:

'Jesus! Do you know what these are?'

Either way she looked surprised at my reaction.

I gathered my breath and explained (possibly condescendingly) that she had brought in three pristine first editions of one of the most influential and original writers of expanded (supernatural and fantasy) fiction in the English language; works that had been a major contribution to the poetic imagination, outside and beyond all the drab parlours of more excitable classic literature.

'Oh! You have heard of him then?' She replied nervously.

'Heard of him!?'

And here I fear I gave her a minor lecture on the importance and meaning of the author's life and work, of his profound influence over H.P. Lovecraft, and how Borges had claimed him as the genius of Magic Realism — all delivered in a frenzy of unhearing enthusiasm, concluding with:

'Where did your grandfather get them?' She turned her gaze downwards at the rudeness of my hysteria.

'My great-grandfather', she corrected.

And then the heavy, thick, Victorian penny started to move, to roll down its convoluted brass track and eventually drop into the waxen ear of the non-listener.

'You mean he IS your grandfather?'

'Great-grandfather', she said again.

And I finally heard what she was saying and what the books on the table meant. And how the core of mystery and the invention of original composition had passed secretly in the blood from the author of the three first editions: Arthur Machen to his great-grand-daughter, Tessa Farmer.

Tessa Farmer and Arthur Machen: Perichoresis

John Sears

I have been amazed by the wonderful burning and the strange fiery colours of the eyes of a single moth, as it crept up the pane outside. Imagine the effect of myriads of such eyes, of the movement of these lights and fires in a vast swarm of moths, each insect being in constant motion while it kept its place in the mass...[1]

Interviewed in 2012, Tessa Farmer spoke of her 'imaginary universe': 'It's really about eating, finding food, hunting.' 'Nothing's ever finished', she ironically concluded, alluding to both her work and its themes.[2] Perpetual cyclical process, the relentless 'unfinishedness' of life even in death, is a key concern of Farmer's art, which constructs a world devoid of the illusory teleologies of human agency, empty of sensible aims and objectives, 'free of morality and individualism', in the words of one critic.[3] Farmer's works imagine in meticulous and grotesque detail the perpetually vicious morbidity of the underbelly of Enlightenment rationalism. Grounded in the material bodies of insects and animals, they enact a corrupt dialectic in which the active principle of life, creation, production, is penetrated and exposed in its negation by the dark, murderous, parasitic workings of swarms of minute supernatural beings — Farmer's monstrously undead corpse-fairies, who collapse the life-death opposition and redefine its movement by hijacking the unwitting bodies of all orders of animated beings, from flies to foxes, to further their own unfathomable ends.

Life, death, and undeath interpenetrate in a complex dance of interdependence limning the sudden perception (as we gaze through magnifying glasses and microscopes) of an alternate and terrifying reality existing within and amidst, parasitic upon, but wholly other to, ours. This complex dance characterises perichoresis — the interpenetration of different entities, their inseparable combination, their mutual indwelling within each other — 'an insidious intrusion', as the title of one of Farmer's animations phrases it. Perichoresis (its contested etymology offers peri, a going around, a circulation, and khoreu, dance, or khora, place) has traditionally described the dance of the Holy Trinity in theological attempts to figure their simultaneous individuation and mutual interdependence. It asserts the presence within one reality of alternate ones — or, in Jacques Derrida's reading of Plato's perichoretic dance in the *Timaeus*, 'a series of mythic fictions embedded mutually in each other'.[4] It also affords a way of understanding some of the ways Farmer's art shares key themes and concerns with the work and life of her great-grandfather, the Welsh writer Arthur Machen.

Born in 1863, Machen's life overlapped by 14 months with that of romantic visionary poet John Clare (1793–1864); Machen died in 1947, the same year Jack Kerouac (1922–1969) set out on the journey that would be recorded a decade later in *On the Road*. This life indicates in its span something of the strange continuities and transformations, the odd, disturbing perichoretic interpenetrations of history, biography, and myth, with which his writings were often concerned. Machen was born Arthur Llewelyn Jones (Machen, adopted as a pen-name, was his mother's surname) in Caerleon-on-Usk in Gwent, site of an Iron Age hill fort and, later, of the Roman fort Isca Augusta; Victorian archaeological works frequently exhumed remnants of both during Machen's childhood. Tennyson wrote sections of his Arthurian poem cycle *Idylls of the King* (1858–85) while staying at Caerleon in 1856, and Arthurian legend as retold by Malory and Chrétien de Troyes sustains the town's claims to a significant place in the mythos. Machen's childhood was thus spent in a deeply palimpsestic historical environment, in which visible and textual traces of former lives and civilisations repeatedly interpenetrated with the burgeoning modernity of mid-Victorian Britain. The effort in his writing to encompass both nevertheless often betrays a strong preference for the imaginative freedoms of the former over the bustling constraints of the latter.

Educated, while his father could afford the fees, at Hereford Cathedral School, Machen subsequently lived as a journalist-writer, first in London and later, on the back of an inheritance, with his wife Amy in the Chilterns. His first book was *An Anatomy of Tobacco* in 1884, but his key works were written through the 1890s, beginning with 'The Great God Pan' in 1894 — 'at the time regarded as scandalous for its implicit sexual content', one critic notes,[5] a scandal Machen referred to as 'a storm in a Tiny Tot's teacup'[6] — and *The Three Impostors* in 1895. As his money ran out, and his first wife developed the cancer that (in 1899) would kill her, he wrote to earn a living and worked for a while as a sub-editor for *Literature* (which eventually became the *TLS*). Famously a champion of spiritual values in opposition to what he perceived as the corrosive contemporary forces of business and science, Machen's writing both drew on, and contrasted with, the popular works of his major contemporaries, Robert Louis Stevenson and Arthur Conan Doyle. His fiction often (for example) makes use of deductive detective work deriving in part from Edgar Allan Poe's Dupin as well as Conan Doyle's Sherlock Holmes to explicate plot developments, and draws formally on the episodic narrative forms favoured by Stevenson; but his texts are distinct from those of Poe and Conan Doyle in tone and style, and in their willingness to allow supernatural elements to interpenetrate the rationalist generic universe of crime and detection.

In one of the first full-length studies of his work, Reynolds and Charlton note that Machen's originality lay partly in another distinct element of his writing: his 'use of background [...] in turning to horrific account scenes that are unmistakably natural and real.'[7] The 'natural and real' elements of Machen's scenic descriptive powers (seen to great effect in the 'Green Book' narrative of 'The White People', published in 1904) derive in part from his awareness of how a particularly acute psychology of fear could be generated through the meticulous construction, within anonymised and integrally unreliable narrative forms, of a profound and meticulously realised sense of the presence of place. Whether the busy streets of London or the winding pathways and tunnels of an isolated woodland landscape, Machen locates his reader firmly in a world experienced as both familiar and uncanny, always potentially mappable and yet sometimes suddenly and disturbingly alienating, 'apt (he writes in 'The Red Hand' [1895]) to suggest the mystical to any one strongly gifted with imagination'.[8]

Marginal to the institutional forms of the Anglo-Catholicism he publicly espoused, Machen nevertheless achieved a strangely popular religious success with his tale 'The Bowmen', published in late September 1914, which entered wartime public consciousness when its themes (of historical return and repetition, of vengeance and retribution) were reified in the public and military imagination as the myth of 'the Angel of Mons', allegedly appearing to guide the British troops to victory at the Battle of the Marne, a fortnight before the tale was published. A major post-war resurgence of interest in his work, particularly in America, enabled him to live amid high society in St John's Wood in the late 1920s. He continued publishing material through the 1930s (often tales that had been written many years before). He and his second wife, Dorothie Purefoy Hudlestone, whom he had married in 1903, retired to Beaconsfield, near Amersham, where Machen died in 1947.

Machen's extensive fictional, critical, and journalistic writings, produced in a variety of different economic and environmental circumstances, inhabit the fringes of British literary modernity, and he constantly struggled to make a literary living. His critical reputation is, for a variety of reasons, somewhat contested, and much of his work is currently out-of-print or available only in limited-print-run collector's editions. He was described in 2012 (by Stefania Forlini) as 'a lesser-known Decadent writer' — an epithet that effectively restricts focus to his output in the 1890s — despite continuing to write well into old age and receiving some serious modernist critical attention later in his lifetime.[9] His most assiduous modern critic, the ubiquitous weird-fiction scholar S.T. Joshi, pays him good attention but nevertheless condemns his oeuvre for its size, content, and form, commenting that:

> Machen's worst flaw — over and above his insubstantial philosophy, his clumsy polemics, his complete lack of narrative skill — is that he wrote too much.[10]

Such criticisms underplay the regional and generic significance of Machen's writing, and ignore how his fiction extends certain Romantic concerns with perception and reliability — the tension between sensibility and intelligibility — into two key specifically modernist features that insist in his work: secular but religiously-evocative experiences of the sublime and the epiphanic (recently analysed by Nicholas Freeman, who distinguishes Machen's versions of epiphany from those of other, more mainstream modernists like James Joyce and Virginia Woolf)[11]; and modernist explorations of the effects of narrative unreliability, such as embedded and found manuscripts, indirectly recounted tales, and incredulous first-hand narratives that defer and delay authorial trust, along with the narrative disorder and incompleteness effected by fragmented or serial-episodic narratives.

This can be seen in *The Three Impostors*, which still seems baffling to Joshi when he discusses it in 2011:

> *But what purpose could Machen have in seemingly dynamiting the seriousness and power of the episodes [...] by putting them in the mouths of dubious characters?*

he asks, with a faint air of despair.[12]

Machen's critical fortunes are currently on the rise. He is a favourite of pop culture icons like Mick Jagger and Mark E. Smith, who recalled his early influences in an interview in 2011:

> *I'd been reading Arthur Machen — 'The Novel of the White Powder.' A great drug book. At night school they gave us E.M. Forster:* A Passage to India. *I found that harder to relate to.*[13]

Machen is tangentially popular with Gothic criticism (although markedly absent from, or only incidentally present in, many of the now-canonical 'Readers' in recent Gothic theory, receiving no mention in, for example, *The Routledge Companion to Gothic*).[14] Critics of *fin de siècle* Gothic, like Kelly Hurley, have drawn attention to the subtler complexities underpinning Machen's apparent dismissal of modern science, noting his perception of it (a perception shared, Hurley argues, by much popular modernist horror and science fiction) rather as 'a liminal art' concerned with 'the unpredictable strangeness of the natural world and the bizarre, shifting nature of the human subject itself.'[15]

Machen's London writings (most notably *The London Adventure* of 1924) are now understood as significant texts in the history of British psychogeography.[16] Writers like Iain Sinclair have celebrated his mappings of the urban landscape, and his explorations of its palimpsestic historical complexities, its layering of experience and event into complex compound texts saturated with compressed cultural meaning — a process he performs also with the border landscapes of his childhood. Machen appears in Sinclair's borderland fiction, *Landor's Tower* (2001), as an avatar of the spirit of place, a crucial figure (alongside the likes of David Jones and Henry Vaughan, the Silurist) of the literary emanations of interstitial space:

> These Welsh borderlands, as Arthur Machen knew, are passages where sights and sounds break through the mantle of unconvinced reality with grail hints, chthonic murmurings, earth spirits and strange atavistic impulses. [...] Exiled in London, he married the gothic horror of the alleys and courtyards he walked so compulsively, the conjurings in suburban villas, with invocations of prelapsarian bliss.[17]

Recent criticism has fruitfully approached Machen as a minor writer (in the Deleuze-Guattarian sense, working in marginal generic forms but in the dominant language of an oppressed minority)[18] and as a writer whose works engage in complex and unsettling ways with questions of deep historical time and cultural memory.[19] Stephen King's recent novel *Revival* (2014) self-consciously reworks 'The Great God Pan', updating its events (in familiar King fashion) to 1960s Maine; King's *Pet Sematary* (1983) draws more indirectly on the geography and structuring events of Machen's 1895 tale 'The Shining Pyramid' (which may also have lent King the title *The Shining*). This theoretical-critical and popular-cultural dance of attention, allusion, influence, and derivation affords the contemporary reader access to a complex, multifaceted version of Arthur Machen, a writer whose autobiographical texts intermingle in curious, unsettling ways with his weird fiction, embodying in formal and thematic patterns the dynamic of perichoresis with which his themes and topics ceaselessly engage.

This engagement is often explicit. At the end of his short story 'N' (1936), Machen's narrator Arnold relates 'in the very heart of London' to two friends 'the story of his researches and perplexities', a tale of looking out of a suburban window and seeing mundane city streets and vehicles, and, on being told to 'Look again', witnessing 'a panorama of unearthly, of astounding beauty [...] which seemed to speak of fairyland itself.' He pauses:

> *And after a pause, he added: 'I believe that there is a perichoresis, an interpenetration. It is possible, indeed, that we three are now sitting among desolate rocks, by bitter streams [...] And with what companions?'* [20]

Perichoresis describes the insistent implication of much of Machen's writing — the sense, never clearly stated but implied, sketched-out without ever being fully coloured-in, that contemporary reality is imperceptibly but irremediably both framed and permeated by the traces of ancient, wholly other, worlds. The writer's task, his work suggests, is to indicate the possibility of perceiving these traces — of looking again at the mundane in order to perceive the extraordinary within it — by generating what Machen called (in his analysis of Stevenson's *Strange Case of Dr Jekyll and Mr Hyde*) 'an outward sign of an inward mystery'. [21] As Donald R. Burleson argues, the 'allegory of reading' offered by 'N' constructs 'London-as-text, [a city] of textual variegation, indeterminacy, polysemy, mystery' — the city as a place subject to endless interpretation and always potentially interpenetrated, transformed, by the otherness of different places imported into it by imaginative force and existing, normally unsuspected, within it. [22]

Machen's perichoretic texts often open and close in framing dialogue, typically between learned and sceptical men disputing experience and its authority. 'The White People' (1904) opens with a dialogue between Ambrose and Cotgrave on sin and evil and their mutual interdependence: 'Evil', Ambrose declares, 'of course, is wholly positive — only it is on the wrong side'. [23] Ambrose's examples of sin — talking animals, singing roses, blossoming stones — signify transgressions of the rule of nature: 'An attempt', as he puts it, 'to penetrate into another and higher sphere in a forbidden manner'. [24] Out of the system of oppositions established in the discussion — good/evil, civilised/natural, human/animal — emerges a third intensified term, 'the true evil [that] differs generically from that which we call evil'. [25] Such evil is embodied in the weird narrative recounted in the anonymously-authored 'Green Book' that contains the narrative framed by this rational debate, where we read a child's extraordinary vision of perichoresis, of the spectacular interpenetration of the transcendental machinery of the universe with that of the perceiving self:

> ... I saw nothing but circles, and small circles inside big ones, and pyramids, and domes, and spires, and they seemed all to go round and round the place where I was sitting, and the more I looked, the more I saw great big rings of rocks, getting bigger and bigger, and I stared so long that it felt as if they were all moving and turning, like a great wheel, and I was turning too, in the middle.[26]

This hallucinogenic and disconcerting trip, echoing Henry Vaughan's Renaissance vision of eternity in 'The World', 'Like a great ring of pure and endless light', and pre-empting W.B. Yeats' Viconian 'Turning and turning in the widening gyre'[27], locates Machen's writing in a visionary tradition that proposes what Edward J. Ahearn calls 'exhilarating if frightening transcendances'.[28]

Dyson and Salisbury, in 'The Inmost Light' (1894), a condensed reworking of 'The Great God Pan', exemplify the tendency to construct contrasting positions, the former feeling 'sometimes positively overwhelmed with the thought of the vastness and complexity of London', the latter reassuring him that 'the mystery of London exists only in your fancy'.[29] Machen blurs together these two distinct world-views, collapsing them as he shades them, gradually and suddenly, so that the ostensibly subtle ideological shift is clearly mapped in the inverted abruptness of the tale's fantasy geography, its 'dead stop' rather than 'soft gradations' as the edge of the city becomes countryside. The events that concern 'The Inmost Light' provide such a moment of graduated abruptness: Dyson perceives behind (not, this time, out of) the window of a common suburban house ('the last house in the row before me') a face, a perception that breaks the surface of suburban convention by indicating an 'insidious intrusion': 'It was the face of a woman, yet it was not human'.[30] With this negative affirmation, the geometry of the real, the tale's anchoring in recognisable space and time, is blown apart:

> *I knew I had looked into another world — looked through the window of a commonplace, brand-new house, and seen hell open before me.*[31]

Such a perichoretic moment, the sudden perception within banal suburban domesticity of some kind of 'hell' which, in that intrusion, is revealed as in some sense always having been there, as latently embedded within and thus always potentially transformative of the fabric of normality, is the key trope of Machen's fiction, and the nature of this perception of 'hell', and its implications for the delicate fabric of the real, are its recurrent concern. It is what links him — via a century of Gothic and horror imagery from popular and high culture, from the divine pig's head of Golding's *Lord of the Flies* to the brutal events of Iain Banks' *The Wasp Factory*, from the swarming monstrous ants of Gordon Douglas' *Them!* to the seething subterranean bucolic of David Lynch's *Blue Velvet* — to Tessa Farmer's infernal insect-machines and silently buzzing horrors.

A fundamental feature of Machen's interpenetrating ancient and modern worlds is the persistence into modern culture of mythically ancient races, the survival in tales and in the popular imagination of ancient peoples, rumoured (Machen's fictions insist) to inhabit yet the hidden spaces, the dark recesses, of the British countryside, and altogether other in their intentions, actions and effects to the roles assigned to them through their official assimilation to the moral literature of childhood. A key link between Machen's work and that of his great-grand-daughter is their shared interest in 'the little people', the folk of faery lore who populate these mythic survivals. Machen had little time for modern reifications of the fairies; he wrote with sceptical contempt of the 'Cottingley Fairy' craze of 1920:

> *This 'fairy' is believed in and commented on by grave men, men of undoubted culture, men of undoubted intelligence — in other*

> *matters, at all events. Nay, serious scientific language is brought in*
> *to explain these in camera fairies: they are invisible to most mortal*
> *eyes, it appears, but the ultra-violet rays perceive them and fix*
> *them on the photographic plate. And their intelligence is measured*
> *by the experts; it is equal to that of the average Newfoundland dog,*
> *or perhaps a little lower. And their business? Skilled and scientific,*
> *they build up the molecules which compose the flowers. There you*
> *are! I believe I should have a mob waiting to see the Hampton Court*
> *Dragons fed — if I placed my cards with a certain discretion.*[32]

— and followed up this sarcastic dismissal with a more measured assertion of his own thoughts on the matter, drawing on anthropological and historical (rather than mystical and pseudo-scientific) conjecture:

> *It is probable, then, that the pre-Celtic inhabitants of these*
> *islands may account for a great deal of fairy tradition; but not,*
> *I think, for all. The fairies are also gods and goddesses of the*
> *old time now diminished in dignity but still potent; and, be it*
> *remarked, always, or almost always, evil.*[33]

Tessa Farmer's *The Coming of the Fairies* (2011) is titled after Conan Doyle's book on the Cottingley Fairies. Farmer's engagement with the fairy myth shares Machen's awareness that its inhabitants are 'evil', scarcely the frilly paper cut-outs of the Cottingley forgeries, and both Machen and Farmer deploy their versions of fairy mythology in order to explore how terrifyingly unrepresentable experiences might be encoded in mythically comprehensible forms.

Machen's versions of 'unrepresentable experiences' centre (in tales like 'The Great God Pan' and 'The White People') on awakening sexuality or Victorian male anxieties about femininity, on the terrifying blurring of natural and human boundaries ('Novel of the White Powder'), and the bewildering interpenetration of real and imagined worlds made possible by new sciences and new orders of knowledge ('The Inmost Light') or strange archaeological discoveries and connected but unaccountable events ('The Red Hand'). Those explored in Farmer's works concern the double interactions of mortality and decay with life and regeneration, the violently destructive forces of the natural world and their paradoxically creative effects. Farmer's biological and anatomical studies motivate her forensic analysis of brutal dynamism, expressed in tableaux that capture moments in an endless cyclical mythos. Where Machen's writings exploit 'found' texts and 'accidental' perceptions of the abysses destabilising rational thought, Farmer's likewise 'found' insect corpses and taxidermied animals are arranged to afford momentary insights into other abysses in which we momentarily perceive the endless fight of life to become death. Farmer's fairies — tiny, malignant entities, motivated by vicious urges — testify to the persistence of uncontrollable forces beneath the veneer of the civil and social, just as Machen's fairy folk bear witness to atavistic persistences, the survival into modernity of powers accrued to things long dead, traces of what he called 'the mad irrationalities which infest the human mind'.[34] Farmer's works echo Machen's in subtle, historically distorted ways traceable through modernist and postmodernist insect genealogies that would include such diverse texts and figures as Wells' *Empire of the Ants*, the Capek Brothers' *Insect Play*, Kafka's Gregor Samsa, Nabokov's extensive writings on butterflies, Cronenberg's *The Fly*, Cindy Sherman' *Fitcher* photographs, and Gunter van Hagen's *Body Worlds* installations. The viewer is invited by such potential connections to discern multiple links and repetitions, just as Machen's writings sound the depths of unrecorded history in their attempts to divine originary traces and their contemporary shadows.

Farmer and Machen are linked, finally, by their shared fascination with theurgical terror, a concern that embeds their works in the ideological fabrics of their respective ages. One of Machen's most powerful tales, 'The Terror' (1917), offers a remarkable evocation of the self-propagating climate of paranoia that engulfs wartime England, descending through layers of official and unofficial censorship and unknowability to trace a series of mysterious murders popularly attributed to a 'sleeping army' of concealed German invaders lurking (like the fairy folk themselves) in the woods and caverns of Britain's margins. The tale's ingenious resolution fuels further the contemporary critical-theoretical significance of his work, evoking as it does a natural world seemingly goaded into fighting back in the most brutally desperate way imaginable against destructive human folly, raising the question of how human and natural worlds interpenetrate each other, and what might be the consequences of such interpenetrations. Frank Schätzing's *The Swarm* (2004) reworks the tenets of Machen's wartime tale as a twenty-first century science fiction narrative, exploring what Slavoj Žižek calls 'the impact the discovery of another intelligent species on Earth might have on us'[35] — an encounter with the otherness embedded within and perichoretically interpenetrating our reality that lies at the heart of Machen's weird tales. Tessa Farmer's fairy nightmares, Machen reworked through Harryhausen, deliberately situate themselves in relation to such SF traditions, intensifying their expression of subterranean cultural anxieties. *Swarm* (2004) may allude to Schätzing's novel, just as *The Wasp Factory* (2013) reprises Banks' 1984 text; her *The Terror*, an installation exhibited in Colchester (2006) and Brighton (2013), repeats the title of her great-grandfather's work, which she discusses in her essay 'Beyond the Veil', in terms that might equally apply to herself:

> *Machen's fairies invariably wreak havoc and commit heinous crimes against humanity. The creatures that we encounter in this strange borderland world, between dreams and death, are horrible and loathsome, responsible for abductions, murders and rape.*

Likewise Farmer's fairies: in her depictions of their monstrous grappling with insects and mammals, we catch a contemporary intimation of the phenomenon that Arthur Machen understood as 'the Little People' — 'Beings of another order from that of man, Beings to be beheld with awe and dread of the spirit'.[36]

Notes

1. Arthur Machen, 'The Terror', *The White People and Other Weird Stories*, edited by S.T. Joshi. (London: Penguin, 2011), 351.

2. Kasia Cieplak-Mayr von Baldegg, 'Taxidermy, Bugs, and Flying Skeletons: The Art of Tessa Farmer': http://www.theatlantic.com/video/archive/2012/10/taxidermy-bugs-and-flying-fairy-skeletons-the-art-of-tessa-farmer/263546/ Accessed 14 January 2015.

3. John Doran, 'Amon Tobin and Tessa Farmer: Control over Nature', *The Quietus* (16 May 2011): http://thequietus.com/articles/06256-amon-tobin-and-tessa-farmer-control-over-nature Accessed 14 January 2015.

4. Jacques Derrida, 'Khora', *On the Name*, edited by Thomas Dutoit, translated by David Wood et al (Stanford: Stanford University Press, 1995), 113.

5. Gary K. Wolfe, 'Fantasy from Dryden to Dunsany', *The Cambridge Companion to Fantasy Literature*, edited by Edward James and Farah Mendlesohn (Cambridge: Cambridge University Press, 2012), 7–20: 18.

6. Machen, *The Autobiography of Arthur Machen* (London: Garnstone Press, 1974, 243.

7. Aidan Reynolds and William Charlton, *Arthur Machen: A Short Account of his Life and Work* (London: The Richards Press, 1963), 49.

8. Machen, 'The Red Hand', *The White People and Other Weird Stories*, 202.

9. Stefania Forlini, 'Modern Narratives and Decadent Things in Arthur Machen's *The Three Impostors*', *ELT* 55:4 (2012), 479–98; 480. S.T. Joshi's 1990 bibliography (see note 10) includes 29 pieces of published critical appreciation of Machen, with works by writers such as John Dickson Carr, M.P. Shiel, Vincent Starrett, Julian Symons, and Carl Van Vechten.

10. S.T. Joshi, *The Weird Tale* (Austin: University of Texas Press, 1990), 17.

11. Nicholas Freeman, 'Arthur Machen: Ecstasy and Epiphany', *Literature & Theology* 24:3 (September 2010): 242–55.

12. Joshi, 'Introduction' to *The White People and Other Weird Tales* (London: Penguin, 2011), xvi.

13. Mark E. Smith, interviewed by Robert Chalmers, *The Independent* (Sunday 13 November 2011): http://www.independent.co.uk/arts-entertainment/music/features/life-lessons-mark-e-smith-on-bullying-the-occult-and-why-stalin-had-the-right-idea-6260036.html Accessed 14 January 2015.

14. Catherine Spooner and Emma McEvoy (eds.), *The Routledge Companion to Gothic* (London: Routledge, 2007).

15. Kelly Hurley, 'British Gothic Fiction, 1885-1930', *The Cambridge Companion to Gothic Fiction*, edited by Jerrold E. Hogle (Cambridge: Cambridge University Press, 2002), 189–208; 192. Hurley echoes Glennis Byron's earlier connection of Machen's work with that of Wilde, Wells, and Marsh, and their shared concern with 'the dissolution of the nation, of society, of the human subject itself', 'Gothic in the 1890s', *A Companion to the Gothic* edited by David Punter (Oxford: Blackwell's, 2001), 133.

16. For recent discussion of Machen's London writings see Joanna Wargen, 'All Eyes are on the City: Arthur Machen's Ethnographic Vision of London', *Literary London: Interdisciplinary Studies in the Representation of London*, 8: 1 (March 2010): http://www. literarylondon.org/london-journal/march2010/wargen.html Accessed 15 January 2014.

17. Iain Sinclair, *Landor's Tower, or The Imaginary Conversations* (London: Granta Books, 2001), 166–7.

18. Jeffrey Michael Renye, *Panic on the British Borderlands: The Great God Pan, Victorian Sexuality, and Sacred Space in the Works of Arthur Machen*. Unpublished PhD Thesis (Temple University, January 2013), 200.

19. Aaron Worth, 'Arthur Machen and the Horrors of Deep History', *Victorian Literature and Culture*, 40 (2012), 215–227.

20. Machen, 'N'. E-text available at: https://ebooks.adelaide.edu.au/m/machen/ arthur/n/ Accessed 12 January 2015.

21. Machen, *Hieroglyphics* (New York: Mitchell Kennerley, 1913), 91.

22. Donald R. Burleson, 'Arthur Machen's 'N' as Allegory of Reading', *Lore* (18 January 2012): http://www.lore-online.com/index.php/component/content/article/43-vault/80-mm4-2 Accessed 19 January 2015.

23. Machen, 'The White People', *The White People and Other Weird Stories*, 112.

24. Ibid., 'The White People', 114.

25. Ibid., 'The White People', 115.

26. Ibid., 'The White People', 123.

27. Henry Vaughan, 'The World', *Metaphysical Poetry*, edited by Colin Burrow (London: Penguin Books, 2006), 220-2; W.B. Yeats, 'The Second Coming', *Selected Poems*. edited by Timothy Webb (London: Penguin Books, 2000), 124–5.

28. Edward J. Ahearn, *Visionary Fictions: Apocalyptic Writing from Blake to the Modern Age* (New Haven: Yale University Press, 1996), 172. Ahearn's book makes no mention of Machen.

29. Machen, 'The Inmost Light', *The White People and Other Weird Stories*, edited by Joshi (London: Penguin, 2011), 3.

30. Ibid., 'The Inmost Light', 6.

31. Ibid.

32. Machen, 'April Fool', *Dog and Duck: A London Calendar, Et Cætera* (London: Jonathan Cape, 1924), 46–7.

33. Machen, 'A Midsummer Night's Dream', *Dog and Duck*, 60.

34. Machen, 'Some February Stars', *Dog and Duck*, 113.

35. Slavoj Žižek, *Absolute Recoil: Towards a New Foundation of Dialectical Materialism* (London: Verso Books, 2013), 13.

36. Machen, 'The Little People', *Dreads and Drolls*. E-text available at: https://ebooks.adelaide. edu.au/m/machen/arthur/dreads-and-drolls/index.html Accessed 17 January 2015.

A Natural History of Tessa Farmer's Fairies
Gavin R. Broad

...they are the dread, and destroyer of other tribes
— Edward Donovan, 1793

Writing about ichneumons in the late eighteenth century, Edward Donovan evoked a savage natural history of parasitoid wasps that lay their eggs inside other insects and eat them alive. According to Donovan, ichneumons 'exist by rapine and plunder, and support their infant offspring on the vitals of larger insects', and he describes the fate of the host insect thus: 'it is now in vain that the unwieldy animal attempts resistance, as all its efforts are but the sport of a savage conqueror'.[1] It is within just such a battlefield that Tessa Farmer's fairies can be located; their niche is one that is familiar to entomologists. Donovan himself could well have been writing about these malicious little fairies. Farmer's art is firmly rooted in the natural world. Her pieces are assembled with the detailed eye of a biologist recording the interactions of the natural world. Like a traditional naturalist, Farmer has spent many hours studying her organisms in their cultural habitat, in museum collections.

This is a brief study of the fairies within the natural world, of their interactions with other creatures and the evolution of their parasitic, host utilisation strategies.

From a scientific perspective, there are several very interesting features of Farmer's art, particularly the incorporation of evolution, attention to anatomical detail, and the adoption of biological pathways from the natural world, such as parasitism and enslavement of other organisms. There are many characteristics that Farmer's fairies share with parasitoid wasps; some of these traits are convergent and coincidental, others are deliberate, in that Farmer has used very real organisms and biology to inform the evolution of her fairies. Prominent links between the fairies and the natural world are the parasitoid wasps, including Donovan's ichneumons. 'Parasitoid' is applied to a particular biology whereby one animal is used by another as food for its offspring, in a way that does not involve the immediate death of the host but does mean its eventual demise. The parasitoid larva starts its life acting like a parasite, extracting nutrition from the body of its host, but ends more like a predator, invariably killing the host. This is a gruesome yet intimate relationship that has played a very important role in shaping ecosystems through the specialised host-parasitoid relationships, and the high mortality rates inflicted on host insect populations.[2] Not all parasitoids are wasps (there are also parasitoid flies, fungi, beetles, etc.) but most of them are. These wasps are not the insects that most people would associate with being wasps but are a diverse assemblage within the insect order Hymenoptera, that includes ants, bees, sawflies and wasps. The parasitoids are classified in many different families and comprise about 50,000 described species, a small fraction of the hundreds of thousands of species that are reckoned to exist. During her residency at the Natural History Museum in 2007, Farmer uncovered some of the diversity of these parasitoids and found that they had a lot in common with her fairies. Evolutionary development of the fairies has since explored some interesting, parasitoid-inspired paths. Creatures such as mosquitoes are used by the fairies to subdue and torment other creatures but I am most interested in the wasps, the organisms that have significantly informed the behaviours of the fairies and which Farmer has described as being the fairies' natural competitors.

Unlike their showier, black and yellow-striped, nest-building cousins, the parasitoid wasps are generally a more unobtrusive part of the fauna. Although the majority of species are unfamiliar to most people, these wasps comprise more than 6,000 species in Britain alone. The basic fact that another organism serves as helpless food for the wasp larva, and that there are many innovative ways in which a host can be utilised and manipulated, has served as inspiration for some of the fairies' maleficent and savagely inventive behaviours. Many extreme host-parasitoid relationships exist in nature and these natural histories are studied, adapted and diced by Farmer. The fairies essentially use other creatures to enable the propagation of other fairies. All sorts of animals are parasitised, enslaved, and dismembered to provide the raw materials for reproduction. Fairies develop in cocoons on fox fur, sometimes in appropriated wasp cocoons. They hybridise to take advantage of long wasp ovipositors (the dual egg-laying organ and sting) to lay eggs in juicy locations, such as in the mouth of a fox (*Little Savages*, 2007; see page 52). None of these strategies would seem too outrageous from the perspective of a parasitoid wasp that needs to utilise hosts efficiently and pragmatically. Sometimes this means ovipositing in the brain of a caterpillar to avoid its immune response, or even ovipositing up the anus of a caterpillar, lodging its egg in the hind gut, which is a physiologically external cuticle and thus without an immune response.

The fairies and their rather sadistic world become more plausible when we observe the realities of the parasitic, predatory and generally manipulative nature of many interactions between known organisms. Given the variety of parasitic interactions extant, there is obviously huge potential for the fairies to evolve in many more directions, co-opting biological processes and other creatures. Enslavement and control of other creatures is a feature of the malevolence of Farmer's fairies. This is a feat achieved by all sorts of parasitic and parasitoid organisms too, albeit often in a more subtle way. Peering closely at the activities in your garden will reveal all manner of intricate, intimate host-parasitoid relationships. One braconid wasp, *Cotesia glomerata*, is a very common parasitoid of the caterpillars of the Large White, and other *Pieris* butterflies. In late summer these caterpillars can be found in great numbers on cabbages and other *Brassica*, and then you can find many examples that have been parasitised. The wasp lays a clutch of eggs within the body of the host caterpillar; the wasp larvae that hatch then eat the caterpillar's haemolymph (blood) and fat but do not consume the muscles or nerves. The caterpillar is better suited to the wasp larvae with its nervous system and muscles in good working order. When the wasp larvae emerge from the host caterpillar their appearance is sudden and the host appears moribund.[3] The wasp larvae are vulnerable at this stage so they rapidly spin thick, silken cocoons in which to pupate. It is at this point that the effect of the wasp larvae on the host caterpillar's brain is revealed; the caterpillar will revive somewhat but remain standing over the *Cotesia* cocoons, spinning extra silk of its own to help protect them and thrashing around at the approach of potential predators (such as the biologist's finger). The caterpillar dies two or three days later, presumably from loss of water and nutrition, but its job is then done as the *Cotesia* larvae have passed through that hazardous moment when they are exposed, nutritious larvae themselves. Examples of mind control and host manipulation by parasitoids are increasingly coming to light, such as recent work showing that a parasitic worm can cause frogs to grow extra legs, or fewer legs, with the result that the frog is significantly less agile and significantly more likely to be eaten by a predator, into which the worm can move for the next part of its life-cycle.[4] Behavioural manipulation of the host can be obvious, such as when the host is a spider that is induced by the parasitoid larva on its thorax to spin a different sort of web to its usual orb web.[5] Parasitoids of spiders have evolved various mechanisms to overcome spiders which are potentially deadly predators to small wasps. Fast reactions and quick-acting paralysing venoms are standard but previously unsuspected behaviours are being discovered as these wasps are studied in the laboratory. Japanese entomologists found that some females of *Zatypota albicoxa* have learnt to avoid the potential dangers of moving

Gavin R. Broad

around a spider's web, locating a spider to parasitise, and instead lie on their backs at the base of the web plucking a support thread in imitation of entrapped prey. The spider is enticed down and, when within reach of the wasp, pounced upon, stung and laid upon.[6] It is tempting to describe all of these innovations as cunning or ingenious but they are no such thing, they are the result of blind evolution. The cunning and ingenuity of Farmer's fairies is real, at least from her imagination, but they have been led there by the precedents of wasps and worms in the wider world.

Over several years, the fairies have evolved more complex relationships with other organisms and evolved more complex morphologies. Clearly they are adapting to ruthlessly use an ever wider palette of creatures to advance the production of more fairies. This could be an abstracted take on our species' rapacious utilisation of natural resources, although it is probably more of a reflection on every organism's prioritising of reproduction and the acquisition of natural resources to enable reproduction; the fairies are able to utilise a wide variety of natural resources through their intelligence, adaptability and tool-making, and, inevitably, these are not put to philanthropic use.

Farmer's fairies use hedgehog and sea urchin spines as spears, claws as grappling hooks, insects' stings and piercing mouthparts. As well as hybrid morphologies, they use such tools to subdue and gain access to their prey and hosts. In the world of parasitoid insects, methods of gaining access to and existing within the bodies of their hosts have evolved in fantastic directions. The diversity of life histories and specialised morphologies is an inspiration behind some of the fairies' more outlandish behaviours. Various groups of wasps have evolved long ovipositors with which to drill through wood and other tough media to reach insect larvae feeding deep within. To accomplish this, zinc and manganese are selectively deposited in high quantities along the cutting edges (or teeth) of the ovipositor, to harden it for the act of drilling.[7] There is no escape from the predations of parasitoid wasps, which utilise a majority of insect species of all life stages as their hosts. Nothing is safe from the fairies either, although they are not constrained by the taxonomy of their hosts. Any creature is fair game, from slugs, sea urchins, sphingid moths, to swans, snakes and swallows.

Gem-like or marvellous inhabitants of the woodlands
heretofore unknown and by most never seem nor dreamt of.[8]

For the early twentieth century American entomologist Alexandre Arsène Girault, the variety of tiny, beautiful parasitoid wasps was astonishing, and a secret, hidden from most people. Farmer's artworks incorporate this beauty and diversity and use the elegant forms of the wasps in the brutal events. In *Little Savages* (2007), a fairy holds a beautiful jewel wasp (Chrysididae) as a drill, forcing it to oviposit into a fox's nose; meanwhile spindly *Ophion pteridis* have their antennae tied together by the fairies. The aesthetic qualities of wasps seldom make it as far as artworks but there is a stunning variety of forms and colours within the group. In a rare example, the French artist Paul Jacoulet incorporates a pelecinid wasp, *Pelecinus polyturator*, in his portrait of a young Melanesian man, *Ephèbe de Metalanim* (1935). In this particular example, the elegant exotic is doubly exotic, as the wasp is a native of America, transposed to South-East Asia. Farmer's creations likewise incorporate elements not naturally juxtaposed.

A web log entry by Emily Goold[9] describes the fairies as constructed of 'raw materials such as roots, mud, and real fairy wings'. It clearly seems feasible to some that fairies could exist. The wings are mostly from Diptera (true flies) and Hymenoptera (wasps and allies) but they look like they really could be from fairies, and many of their original owners are almost as fantastical. The elegant, narrow-waisted forms of ophionines are a good match to the fairy anatomy and they have been hybridised extensively by the fairies, as seen in *Little Savages* and several subsequent pieces. From a purely natural historical perspective, these artworks are fascinating to pick through in identifying all the creatures that have been incorporated.

Attention to anatomical detail is very important; the artworks grab our attention and rather disturb, partly by the fact that these events could be real. Farmer's painstaking observation is made very apparent in the pencil drawings of real specimens from the collections of the museum, that take a very long time to produce, from staring down a microscope at details of the specimen for hours at a time. Resulting pieces such as *Sphingidae parasitised by Rogadinae braconid wasps* (2007) and *Cocoons of microgastrine braconids* (2007), are precise yet soft, executed in pencil, and are faithful recreations of specimens; or, rather, specimens in a museum collection. The distinction is important as the specimens in a collection are laid out in particular ways and are there as snapshots of nature. Mischievous elements, such as the missing caterpillar in *Cocoons...* and the knotting together of very long ichneumonid ovipositors in *Apechoneura nigritarsis* (2007), hint at the fairies at work in the collections, making unseen mischief. Farmer was inspired by the idea of the fairies infesting the Natural History Museum; an all-too-real possibility for certain pest insects such as *Anthrenus* beetles and clothes moths that invade the collections of dried, pinned insects.

The fairies are imbued with parasitoid qualities but they also physically take on the bodies of parasitoid wasps. Going a step further than the parasitoids of reality, the fairies appropriate parts of the bodies of their victims, incorporating these wholesale into their chimeric bodies. The most horrifying thing about these creatures is their humanoid aspect, with a distinct human morphology, especially a skull. This corrupted, skeletal humanity imposed on insect dimensions, and often part-insect physiognomy, imparts a wilfully malicious direction to their actions. Whereas parasitoid wasps use their hosts to produce the next generation of wasps, the fairies seem to be going much further than this in manipulating all sorts of creatures towards greater ends than reproduction alone.

Farmer's fairies started off comparatively large but rapidly shrank, miniaturisation being a frequent evolutionary response of parasites and parasitoids. Evolution has been speeded up in the world of Farmer's art; the fairies miniaturised quickly and have diverged into various morphotypes. It is very tempting to place one of the hybrid fairy wasps in the Natural History Museum's collection for future generations to encounter and wonder at. A wider spectrum of hosts and host stages become available to smaller parasitoids, such as insect eggs. There are many more eggs of insects than there are larvae, pupae or adults, due to inevitable mortality, so this resource has been tapped by guilds of tiny parasitoids such as Trichogrammatidae and the beautiful little Mymaridae, or fairy flies. Huber and Noyes[10] describe some mymarids only around a tenth of a millimetre and discuss the potential lower size limits of flying insects. What are the lower size limits of Farmer's fairies? They are not so constrained by biology, being very adaptable and attacking a wide range of other organisms. Farmer does not use a microscope when working sculpturally, so there is clearly potential here for much smaller fairies, interacting at a much smaller scale with tiny creatures. The limiting factor is probably the ability of the viewer to see and comprehend what is happening in these busy scenes. Farmer has spent many hours examining and drawing wasps down a microscope; how much more could be revealed with magnification of the fairies themselves?

Given the extreme miniaturisation of some parasitoid wasps, how many evolutionary niches are potentially available to the fairies? Life stages such as the eggs of other insects, insect larvae deep within wood, beneath the soil, mammals, reptiles, all manner of marine creatures; are these all fair game? Strategies such as polyembryony (the laying of one egg that multiplies into many, sometimes thousands, of wasp larvae within the host) or of hyperparasitising parasitoid larvae already within a host: these are methods of efficiently utilising resources, commonly practiced in gardens, fields and hedgerows, where it would not be surprising to see the fairies taking their places alongside the wasps. Farmer's dioramas seem to happen in the real world. Her attention to biological and anatomical detail is part of what makes working with her so rewarding for a scientist. The fairies seem a natural component of an everyday scene of death; in *A Prize Catch* (2010) a dead blue tit is surrounded by fly puparia from maggots that have consumed the flesh of the corpse, but the fairies are competitors and predators, carving up the bird corpse and capturing the flies that emerge from the puparia. It all seems rather plausible. What role would such creatures play in an ecosystem that they invaded? Thanks to their humanoid construction, you get the impression that they could be bad news. Even the more fantastical tableaux of enslavement, such as *The Insectary* (2007), involve fairy behaviours that are not too far removed from the grimly fascinating reality of parasitoid wasps. The beautifully taxidermied, life-like rat in *The White Lie* (2011) could well be running across the floor of the gallery, with parasites in its fur.

The grounding of Farmer's art in reality, as if these scenes could really be playing out around our feet, was one of the features that first struck me. Malevolent things happen in hedgerows, gardens, in the air, to all manner of poor creatures. The reality of Farmer's work is anchored in the fates of animals that are often horrifically killed by other animals, enslaved, eaten alive, used. This aspect of their lives is certainly reflected in Farmer's work. Charles Darwin famously considered the life history of a parasitoid wasp to be good evidence for the lack of a god, saying in a letter to a botanist, Asa Gray, 'I cannot persuade myself that a beneficent and omnipotent God would have designedly created the Ichneumonidae'.[11] The main difference between the authentic zoology and Tessa Farmer's dioramas seems to lie in the filtering of human emotion, the ascribing of malice to her fairies, whereas in the hedgerows and gardens around us, very similar things happen, but impassively; grisly death is a fact of life for most organisms.

What are the potential future evolutionary trajectories for the increasingly sadistic fairies? Delving into more microscopic realms would open up a whole other, paradoxically vast world of organismal relationships. Utilising the nests of social insects and enslaving thousands or millions of their inhabitants seems to be a developing trend as witnessed by the horde of ants overwhelming a moorhen in *The Demise of the Tristan Moorhen* (2012). What would ensue if the fairies started colonising the larger wasp nests? They are already overpowering giant swans and pythons...

Notes

1. Edward Donovan, *The Natural History of British Insects; explaining them in their several states, with the periods of their transformations, their food, economy, etc. Together with the history of such minute insects as require investigation by the microscope. The whole illustrated by coloured figures, designed and executed from living specimens* (London: F. and C. Rivington, 1793).

2. They are usually insects but a few other arthropod groups, particularly spiders, also serve as hosts. H. Charles J. Godfray, *Parasitoids: Behavioural and Evolutionary Ecology* (Princeton: Princeton University Press, 1994).

3. Some gruesome footage of *Cotesia glomerata* larvae emerging from a *Pieris brassicae* larva can be seen here: http://www.youtube.com/watch?v=cysBOZtXFeA&feature=youtu.be Accessed 19 May 2015.

4. B.A. Goodman and P.T.J. Johnson, 'Ecomorphology and disease: cryptic effects of parasitism on host habitat use, thermoregulation, and predator avoidance', *Ecology*, 92 (2011): 542–548.

5. W.G. Eberhard, 'Under the influence: webs and building behaviour of *Plesiometa argyra* (Araneae, Tetragnathidae) when parasitized by *Hymenoepimecis argyraphaga* (Hymenoptera, Ichneumonidae)', *The Journal of Arachnology*, 29 (2001): 354–366.

6. K. Takasuka, and R. Matsumoto, 'Lying on the dorsum: unique host-attacking behaviour of *Zatypota albicoxa* (Hymenoptera, Ichneumonidae)', *Journal of Ethology*, 29 (2011): 203–207.

7. D.L.J. Quicke, P. Wyeth, J.D. Fawke, H.H. Basibuyuk, and J.F. Vincent, 'Manganese and zinc in the ovipositors and mandibles of hymenopterous insects', *Zoological Journal of the Linnean Society*, 124 (1998): 387–396.

8. A.A. Girault, *Some gem-like or marvellous inhabitants of the woodlands heretofore unknown and by most never seen nor dreamt of* (Brisbane: private publication, 1925).

9. Emily Goold (2011): http://emilygoold.blogspot.co.uk/2011/02/tessa-farmer.html Accessed 19 May 2015.

10. J.T. Huber and J.S. Noyes, 'A new genus and species of fairyfly, *Tinkerbella nana* (Hymenoptera, Mymaridae), with comments on its sister genus *Kikiki*, and discussion on small size limits in arthropods', *Journal of Hymenoptera Research* 32 (2013): 17–44.

11. Letter from Charles Darwin to Asa Gray (22 May 1860): https://www.darwinproject.ac.uk/letter/DCP-LETT-2814.xml Accessed 19 May 2015.

A Short History of Fairy Painting, 1768–1901
Gail Nina Anderson

As is traditional, the fairies weren't invited to the feast and turned up later determined to be troublesome. (Actually it was originally the goddess Eris who didn't get invited to the wedding celebrations of Thetis and Peleus, so took a huff, threw a golden apple and was ultimately responsible for the Trojan War. That's another story, but real fairies certainly inherited that spiteful streak). Their origins and identity in folklore, however, are dealt with elsewhere. In this chapter I offer a survey of their entry into visual culture, where the medium inevitably moulds the message and the fairy-folk take on shapes which still define them in modern popular imagery.

If, instead of a social celebration, we substitute glorification in the visual arts, we will swiftly see that the fairy does, indeed, only get invited in late in the day, when the tropes of conventional iconography need new blood and folklore becomes an acceptable source — or rather you won't see, because until the late eighteenth century the fairy folk are decidedly absent. This means they remain un-visualised, a presence spun out of words and stories, encountered by the (usually unlucky) few but not actually represented. There are sound socio-economic reasons for this: fairy lore was unofficial, not part of a religion or incorporated into an educational system based mainly on classical languages and ideas. Long before the term was coined in 1846, fairies were part of 'folklore', the ever-shifting pattern of oral traditions that rarely got written down. True, these stories might fuel the elegant, courtly literature of Edmund Spenser or Michael Drayton — they might even be placed centre stage in a William Shakespeare play, designed to be appreciated as much by the unlettered groundlings as by a knowing aristocratic audience — but they didn't get painted. At a period when most significant works of art would have been specifically commissioned by the artist's (necessarily wealthy) customers, it was unlikely they would request the representation of something their kitchen-maids chattered about, something that belonged to the world of credulous country bumpkins and old wives.

The fairies might, of course, claim some kinship to the demons and devils who, as part of an official theological framework, did enjoy a long tradition of visibility in Christian art. Varying in size and usually shown as human/animal hybrids, demons certainly gave artists such as Hieronymus Bosch and Pieter Breughel the chance to exercise their darker imaginings. Unlike fairies, however, such creatures don't embody the mystery of an undefined alternative, rarely glimpsed and never officially recognised. They are by definition there to horrify and their natural environment is hell, but in terms of visualisation they do offer an ancestry for some of the more disturbing denizens of the fairy world. It might be noted, though, that the iconographic anxieties which informed post-Reformation Protestant culture made religious themes very rare in British art until a revival of interest during the nineteenth century. The devils of earlier centuries make their triumphant reappearance not as a matter of belief but in the context of antiquarian and art historical interest.

Even when wealthy patrons were not commissioning images of fairies (or, for that matter, demons) exceptions to their invisibility did begin to be found, unsurprisingly, at the disregarded cheaper end of picture-making, where crude woodcuts adorned printed chapbooks, pamphlets and ballads. It's among the ephemera of the printing industry that fairies first make an appearance, so quite possibly there were once more images of them going around at a penny apiece but long since discarded and decayed — an inexpensive piece of paper doesn't get cherished in the same way as a framed painting, especially when it has a practical secondary use for wrapping or wiping. Fairies do not themselves coincide with the invention of the printed book, but the necessity to draw them with something other than words probably does.

The edition of *Robin Goodfellow, His Mad Pranckes, and Merry Jests, Full of Honest Mirth, and a Fit Medicine for Melancholy* published in London in 1628 (an earlier edition must have been known to Shakespeare, for the character of Puck clearly has its source here) is a good example of the unattributed chapbook, a collection of tales and rhymes recounting the mischievous exploits of a fairy-human hybrid whose roots lie in the depths of oral tradition. Significantly, it has a crude woodcut frontispiece which demonstrates the difficulty of finding a form for fairies. Robin/Puck is shown as a bearded dancing satyr, complete with goat's legs, horns, and notably erect penis. He wears a hunting horn and carries a taper and broomstick, which suit well his persona in folklore. The anonymous artist, however, has gone to a recognisably classical model, perhaps Pan himself, not just a benign nature god but the personification of a natural world where humanity may be irrelevant, an alien environment that breeds 'panic'. The fact that Pan's features were pressed into service when it came to providing a face and form for the Devil adds worrying depths to what really should be a jolly image of a meddling sprite — Farmer's skeletal fairies would certainly feel at home in his realm. Behind him a seated piper plays while a cat (?) sits up and an owl flies above, indicating that this should be read as a night scene. Round him dances a circle of tiny figures, crudely depicted in silhouette but clearly wearing contemporary costume. Are these human worshippers of Robin/Pan/Satan, dwarfed by his stature, or is this an early representation of fairies?

Another woodcut looks to be of roughly the same vintage, but has become detached from any text, so details of date and meaning are effectively lost. An even cruder piece of work, it has a disturbing air of Enid-Blyton-meets-folklore about it. There is a charming whimsy about the little folk populating their landscape, yet their very presence redefines that landscape as dangerous territory, the mundane treacherously informed by the uncanny. Against a hilly background, eight figures, male and female and all in contemporary dress, dance in a ring. A spotted toadstool in the foreground suggests that they are tiny. To the left a little hillock boasts a door; to the right the foliage of a tree reveals a grinning face or mask, perhaps a Green Man. Is this a magical landscape where the fairies dance out those mushroom-spore circles traditionally called 'fairy rings'? Without context it remains enigmatic (the possibility of a satirical meaning cannot be rejected) but at face value it suggests that this might be the way fairies are seen before 'high art' gets at them — solid little wingless beings, not only human in appearance but also properly dressed. (Indeed, the women, with their steeple hats, could still do service as illustrations of the fairy godmother type).

While not exactly sinister, neither are these the gossamer-winged, child-friendly fairies of later popular culture. Like Farmer's fairies they are small (in folklore, fairies come in a variety of models, from tiny to human scale) and flourish in a natural setting, but their clothes suggest that they are viewed as little people.

It's the coming of an 'exhibition culture' that makes the fairy a visual necessity—specifically, the establishment of the Royal Academy in London in 1768 ushers them into the light. An art establishment that had relied on the expectations of the patron (which had usually centred on portraits, landscapes and more portraits) now vastly expanded its iconographic range as artists rose to the challenge offered by regular public exhibitions. On walls crowded with contemporary art, new sorts of subjects would catch the eye of the viewer and (importantly) the reviewer. Originality and imagination became newly valued, as history, literature and The Bible were trawled for motifs and characters. Classical subjects at first represented an intellectual pinnacle, but as the Age of Reason came to an end there was a reaction against this tradition, and a move towards more northern themes. Add to this the fashionable status of the English theatre, with immensely influential actor/manager/playwright/self-promoter David Garrick's virtual canonisation of Shakespeare, and off the back of the Bard the fairies hop onto the walls of the R.A. and its competitors. These are the fairies of folklore but at a couple of removes, translated by Shakespeare into stage characters and now given forms that might reflect theatrical performance (in which case they would be human scale and clothed) or might set free the fancy of the artist to find new shapes. The Swiss-born painter, Henry Fuseli (1741–1825), led the way in finding the weird in Shakespeare, painting Macbeth's witches, the ghost of Hamlet's father, Caliban and Ariel from *The Tempest* and the fairies from *A Midsummer Night's Dream*. The concept of non-human spirits set the painter free from the limitations of visual rationality. His three paintings of *Titania and Bottom* show realistic scale undermined and Shakespearean narrative gleefully embellished. The queen may be classically nude, graceful and perhaps half-scale to her donkey-headed human lover, but her attendants range from bare breasted ballet-dancers with a hint of the dominatrix to dwarfish, child-like figures, grotesque little gnomes and tiny, Michaelangelesque muscular figures small enough (in the Tate painting) to stand on Bottom's hand. Of course, Shakespeare's text had already created fairies who, however they must have looked on stage, seem simultaneously to be human-oised and tiny, insect-like creatures (Moth, Cobweb, Mustard Seed), small enough to do combat with bees to steal their honey-bags. Fuseli's paintings explore these hints — the Tate version, *Titania and Bottom*, first exhibited 1789, features a smirking child whose head is topped with moth-wings, while the Winterthur picture, *Titania Awakening*, exhibited in 1791, has a tiny figure held, as though suckling, to the breasts of a languorous female with an incongruously contemporary hairstyle, as the ass's head is held aloft and the sleeping Bottom is menaced by an unpleasant little goblin on a swooping horse (reminiscent of Fuseli's own *The Nightmare*, exh. R.A. 1782). Though they may swirl aloft, true to folklore his fairies lack wings, except for the disturbingly muscular little male nude who dances with a tiny lady in the foreground of the Zurich painting. Lacking a human cranium he has the head and antennae of a moth, with wings spreading out behind his extended arms.

Nothing else quite so perverse appears in this first generation of fairy pictures, though Fuseli's friend William Blake (1757–1827), created an unnerving apparition at the other end of the size scale in one of his watercolours illustrating Milton's *Il Penseroso and L'Allegro* (1645). The 'lubber fiend' of the text is obviously one of those useful hob-goblins who flail vast amounts of grain in return for a bowl of cream and a night by the fire, but Blake imagines this domestic brownie as a huge, transparent, naked figure, holding bowl and flail, stretching and yawning as he streams up into the sky where dawn is about to break. Dwarfed by his immense scale, a small cottage is shown with an apparently transparent wall so that we can see inside to where several tiny, wingless, naked figures prance around a sleeper, over the foot of whose bed someone stands, proffering — the composition suggests that fairies might, indeed, be the stuff of nightmares.

From such promisingly sinister beginnings, the artistic fairy gets quickly tamed into something altogether more viewer-friendly and characteristically delicate, feminine and bewinged. Romantic ballets such as *La Sylphide* (1832) and *Giselle* (1841) helped fuel their identification with lissom young women, wafting around in flowers and gauze. For reasons dictated by taste more than tradition, in art fairies were often shown naked, and allowed the artist more latitude than most nude subjects. The excuse wasn't simply that they were creatures of the imagination, but that they belonged to a natural realm without shame or soul, so could frolic with animal innocence. This led to some remarkably (if unadmitted) sexualised depictions, but the glamorous, beautiful fairy did sometimes co-exist with the more sinister and worrying goblin type. Daniel Maclise (1806–1870), a favourite painter of Queen Victoria's (indeed, she purchased the picture under discussion), painted a moment from de la Motte Fouqué's immensely popular fairy novella *Undine* (1811) where the lovely water sprite of the title is riding with her human lover through a forest peopled by other supernatural creatures. These include sprightly little nude men, shown for some reason as nattily bearded and bald, scrambling out of the way of the horses or communing with squirrels in the trees. These are presumably the gnomes or underground elementals mentioned in the novel, which takes a Paracelsian view of the supernatural. Also from the 1840s are the two *Titania and Oberon* paintings by Scottish artist Sir Joseph Noel Paton (Fig 4: see colour insert), in which conventions of scale are happily subverted as the exquisitely classicised fairy monarchs are seen with much larger humans and a huge entourage of smaller fairies in a variety of sizes. While the females all share a conventionalised beauty, among the males there are more grotesque, goblin-like figures, lurking in the shadows of river-banks and trees. In the *Reconciliation*, minute figures thrust a spear at a terrified baby owl, while *The Quarrel* has an old man being tumbled into a stream, an ugly, red-capped figure being propitiated by tiny men, a threatening spider, a butterfly harnessed by a gleeful elf and a beautiful girl feeding a lizard from a bowl held suggestively on her lap. Despite their gauzy wings, these fairies are part of a natural world of snails and slugs, damp, dangerous places and inter-species combat, in a scenario presided over by a herm of Pan. This classical deity (appropriate, of course, for the Athenian setting of Shakespeare's play) offers a get-out clause for Victorian viewers. Paton's fairies belong to the wild woods of pagan imaginings, which no doubt excuses their over-riding preoccupation with courtship and caresses, not to mention the sense that they follow some less humane agenda wherever they lurk just out of sight in the shadows. Of course, these are not really the nymphs of the classical world — like Shakespeare, Paton has managed to fuse a culturally high-toned, Graeco-Roman setting with many more local aspects of British fairy-lore. One small detail shows a remarkable nod to the latter — *The Quarrel* includes, contrasting visibly with her pearly-white companion, a small brown-skinned brunette wearing strings of red beads and balancing an insect on her hand. Paton produced a small oil study showing just this detail, and entitled it *The Indian Boy's Mother*. The supernatural plot of *A Midsummer Night's Dream* hinges on Oberon's and Titania's rival claims to a little Indian boy, son of a human devotee of the latter, who died in childbirth. If Paton's exotic beauty is the boy's mother, then she is dead. That the fairy-folk might be the dead is a long-persisting notion that manages to hover alongside Christian belief, even in an officially Christian culture. Paton's awareness of the darker threads of folklore (particularly Scottish traditions, which he may well have picked up directly from oral sources) surfaces in a later picture, *The Fairy Raid: Carrying off a Changeling, Midsummer Eve* (1867). This is not classical — instead of Pan, presiding over the moonlight raid is a group of standing stones and the fairies (the usual mixture of the beautiful and grotesque) are dressed in a conventionalised mediaeval fashion. A beautiful, fair-haired queen carries on her horse a chubby, oversized human baby while pretty, blonde toddlers dance alongside her. These are presumably, like the new baby, children who have been taken by the fairies, with ill-favoured replacements, or changelings, left for their parents to find. The painting is the epitome of romantic, nostalgic Victorian-Celtic imaginings, but in the historical light of a genuine belief in changelings and an often violent response to the 'replacement' child, this is one of the most sinister of fairy pictures.

While Paton's art is often termed Pre-Raphaelite, the members of the P.R.B largely avoided painting fairies for reasons obvious within their artistic philosophy — if you make a point of painting directly from nature, where do you find your fairy models? The major exception is John Everett Millais' 1850 painting *Ferdinand Lured by Ariel*. Like *A Midsummer Night's Dream*, *The Tempest* often provided a literary excuse for painting acceptable supernatural themes, with Ariel usually portrayed as feminised and sprite-like. Millais painted him as a greenish child, apparently seated in mid-air, naked except for the carapace of his transparent green wings folded around him, and apparently supported on a floating circle of stunted, green, bat-winged goblins. Though sinister in appearance (William Michael Rossetti described them as 'vegetable bats'), Ariel and the goblins do nothing more alarming than confuse Ferdinand (to whom they are invisible) by knocking off his hat and providing unseen music. Despite a taste for the uncanny, the more poetically imaginative strand of Pre-Raphaelitism, descending through Rossetti to Burne-Jones and his followers, generally eschewed such grotesqueness. Instead their medieval yearnings found expression in Arthurian subjects where wizards and enchantresses add a Romantic glamour to tales of doomed love and chivalric ideals.

By the mid-nineteenth century fairies were definitely back on the literary and artistic agenda, given a boost by the immensely popular translations of *Grimm's Tales*,[1] and the start of a whole industry of folklore gathering and commentary, such as Thomas Keightley's *The Fairy Mythology* (1828). Comparatively few 'fairy tales', however, feature fairies as such, and with only occasional exceptions (Maclise's *Cinderella* for example, or Burne-Jones' *Briar Rose* series) they proved less attractive to painters than Shakespearean and Arthurian sources had done. Small-scale illustrations might, however, explore the more sinister creatures of these tales — George Cruikshank's contributions to the 1823 English translation of *Grimms' Fairy Tales* includes (for the story *Jorinda und Jorindel*) a crabbed, cruel little-old-lady fairy who cages the birds into which she has transformed young people, while his *Rumpelstiltskin* presents a dark, furious little manikin. The nastiness is undercut, though, by an element of humour, typical of the Victorian identification of the grotesque with the funny. If viewed in relation to such imagery, Farmer's work too reveals a cruel streak of humour in the absurdity of her non-dead dead things, tiny encapsulations of ferocious energy. Unlike the Grimms' illustration they offer no narrative context for their furious exploits, inviting our own fantasies of contextualisation while evading attempts to pin them down.

Perhaps pinning down is a key link to the Victorian mind-set, where a second environment for tiny creatures from the natural world was the collector's cabinet.[2] Farmer's fairies offer a belligerent response to such human colonisation. Far from providing a tool for easy assimilation as specimens or as pretty little oddities, their small scale only makes them more uncanny and perverse.

Miniaturisation, however, was one artistic route that Victorian fairies would take. A gentler version of them as 'the little folk' was popularised by graphic artist Richard (Dickie) Doyle (1824–83; for example Fig 9: see colour insert), illustrator not only of fairy tales but also of *Punch*. Perhaps the latter connection explains the element of satire that creeps into his own volume *In Fairyland: A Series of Pictures from the Elf World* (1869), where graceful fairies are accompanied by mischievous elves and caricatural, moustachioed, little men rather in the style of Mr. Punch himself. Doyle's illustrations help establish the tradition within which Farmer's creatures also exist, depicting energetic little creatures ready to tame birds and insects. They pull that tradition in another direction, however, by presenting the fairy (still somewhat disturbing at this stage) as suitable fare for the nursery. Though still having an edge of oddness to it, and lacking the cloying sweetness and sentimentality of later works intended for children, *In Fairyland: A Series of Pictures from the Elf World* was clearly meant to amuse young readers. Fairies were not just visualised as denizens of the natural world (later works such as Cicely Mary Barker's *Flower Fairy* books, published between 1923 and 1955, would emphasis this to the extent that they function as botanical illustrations as much as fairy characterisations) but also as creatures of the untrammelled imagination. To believe in them was part of an irrational mind-set that was suitable for the infant world-view but hardly appropriate to adult reasoning, where an interest in fairies had to be categorised into safety by such labels as art, literature, folklore etc. Imagination, except in the necessary fantasies of the developing young, should be exercised with such caution that it might enchant the reader/viewer/thinker, but never run away with them. At the same moment that fairies become infant-friendly (which in folklore they are certainly not), they also become sinister indicators of imagination dangerously out of control. There was an indication of this within Doyle's own family. His younger brother, Charles Altamont Doyle (1832–93), father of Sir Arthur Conan Doyle, suffering from alcoholism and depression to the extent that he was institutionalised for the last 12 years of his life, peopled his drawings and watercolours with fairies, goblins and the occasional skeleton, which could be seen as the products of his disturbed mental state. His poignant watercolour *Meditation: Self-Portrait* (1885–93) now in the V&A, shows a worried Doyle at the mercy of his imagination, seated in his moon-lit study while goblins prowl like cats around him.

A better-known case in which fairy paintings are seen, in the light of the artist's medical history, to reveal a sinister implication of an imagination out of control is that of Richard Dadd (1817–86). Dadd, coming from a family cursed with mental health problems, underwent a crisis that led him, while in a delusional state, to murder his father in 1843. Apprehended, he spent the rest of his life in Bethlem Hospital and

Broadmoor, where he painted (among other subjects) *The Fairy Feller's Master-Stroke* (1855–64; Fig 5: see colour insert) and *Contradiction: Titania and Oberon* (1854–58), both works of obsessional and idiosyncratic detail, neither seen in public until the twentieth century. However, Dadd had been a highly promising professional artist before his health failed and, in the early 1840s, had exhibited the much more conventional fairy subjects *Titania Sleeping* (1841), *Come unto these Yellow Sands* (1842) and *Puck* (1841), none of which attracted any contemporary comment to indicate that they were seen as strange or disturbing. Now, however, the power of hindsight means that even these unexceptional academic pictures must reveal that Dadd was already 'away with the fairies' — when *Puck*, which shows the infant Puck seated on a toadstool, was recently acquired by the Harris Museum and Art Gallery Preston, it was observed that: '[t]he dark undertones of the piece are thought to reflect Dadd's turbulent mindset'.[3]

In fact, even the Tate's *The Fairy Feller's Master-Stroke*, the best-known of Dadd's 'mad' paintings, has content no more sinister than might be found in, say, the works of Dickie Doyle — a sturdy workman raises his axe to a hazel nut, watched by a variety of onlookers. Varying in scale, the figures include contemporary types, neckless, dwarfish grotesques, dashing individuals in historical costume, full-bosomed young women, and tiny elves. It creates a moment of frozen action, where the only activity comes from three trumpet-players (one of them a winged insect). What makes the scene disturbing is the visual density of this microcosmic world, where a flowery bank can contain a whole society of strangely various beings, half-hidden by the grasses and tendrils which overlay our view.

Contradiction: Oberon and Titania (1854–58) has a more familiar subject but a wider range of odd details. Here the leafy setting also incorporates an elaborate antique structure, with a processional walkway along which warriors (accompanied by a cymbal-clashing satyr) carry the carcass of a beast. Differences of scale are magnified here, with microscopic beings active among the undergrowth. In the largest group, a stout Titania, classically but substantially draped, confronts a vaguely Assyrian-looking Oberon accompanied by a sly, devilish Puck. The scene is familiar but the details hint at a world of mysteries beyond Shakespeare's drama. In the foreground, winged figures struggle in what looks like a fight between good and evil angels, while a satyr/centaur takes aim at an insect, and over all hangs a green-veined mineral egg. While the foliage framing the figures in this oval composition is mostly dry, with several pine cones indicating a wintry setting, it still includes some flowers in bloom and a remarkably realistically painted butterfly. Dadd's visually unorthodox fairies may stand as symbols of a dangerously uncontrolled imagination, but it would be just as valid to say that they are sinister because they give shape to what *A Midsummer Night's Dream* hints at — a whole world existing in the interstices of our awareness, intimately linked to what we think of as the 'natural' order of things, which order, as in the play, is shifting awry.

The artist who best conveys what worries us about fairies is John Anster Fitzgerald (1823–1906), despite the fact that, at first glance his exquisite, colourfully-dressed creatures might be personifications of the flowers whose petals they wear. Their impassive, alienating prettiness indicates that they belong to a different order of being — they may consume a jewelled feast from a mushroom table or float in a pristine water-lily boat, but any proto-Disney cuteness is undercut by their doll-like inhumanity. And, yes, they have inherited the spiteful streak — they take over a bird's nest, enchain a robin and hunt down a white mouse with vindictive glee. They can also die — *The Fairy's Funeral* echoes a theme familiar in folklore, the echo of a first-hand sighting passed down orally and here transformed into a sparkling flower-garden of grief. Look more closely at Fitzgerald's work, though, and the full development of its other-worldliness strikes you, as attendant figures reveal multiple eyes or insect-like antennae, noses that extend to form harps or trumpets and bodies that morph from tree-trunks or clamber into stolen eggs. That last is a clue — Fitzgerald must have been looking at the paintings of Hieronymus Bosch, where all hell breaks loose in a cacophony of wildly inventive demons. Fitzgerald's fairy grotesques are the hybrid creatures who, in another context, would be the Devil's minions — and far from being amusing, they are genuinely repulsive. He carried this idea further in a series of paintings on the theme of dreaming, obviously inspired at one level by Fuseli's *The Nightmare* but also populated by Boschian demons from the unconscious mind. In *The Artist's Dream* the sleeper's vision of painting a beautiful fay is undercut by the hideous, semi-transparent goblins that hover around him. More disturbing versions show a young girl whose dreams of romance and adventure are spun by the horrible creatures that throng around her, playing the music of her sleep. These are the fairies of nightmare — in one version there is a definite suggestion of some potion drunk — the demons who once threatened only the damned now re-invented as products of the untrammelled imagination of the dreamer. We all, perhaps, carry our own fairies/demons, and they are not always welcome companions.

If the Victorians could play on the concept of 'fairy' as anything from an innocent flower-being to a demon of the mind, Farmer's aggressive little skeletons have expanded on the idea of a world which is both this and other, suggesting a hitherto-undiscovered, disconcertingly Darwinian aspect of 'nature red in tooth and claw', in which they fill an environmental niche. With this line from *In Memoriam*, Tennyson struggled with the idea that 'nature' might no longer be represented as the benign reflection of divine order, having been re-cast by science as something wasteful, violent and impersonal. If this harsh, reluctant conceptualisation allows for any uncanny denizens, Farmer's fairies fit right in. Part of their potency, however, comes not from their Victorian roots but from a glorious clash with our contemporary desire to re-assimilate nature via romantic notions of sympathy and cohesion. If New Age spirituality has, in recent years, re-imagined the fairy as a politically-correct symbol and protector of this unspoiled nature, Farmer's creatures are eco-warriors of quite a different sort. Though their bones suggest that these are dead things, there is something remarkably potent about their gleeful hunting and concentrated energy, hinting that all life is also a matter of death. They come from a world of cocoons and twigs, fungus and decay, where, between the slimy and the desiccated, new shapes slide into an alarming vitality. Despite their tiny size, you would be very unlucky to encounter a swarm of them.

The most worrying thing about fairies might be that they are there at all, largely unseen but a constant threat to both a rational world-view and a conventionally-religious one. They are things that shouldn't be, unaccounted for by science or doctrine — and even among the more categorically-generous ideas of folklore and oral tradition, their status fluctuates alarmingly. They could be the dead, fallen angels, the relics of an ancient race, forgotten gods or simply another dimension of beings that interacts with our own. Visualising them is a way of containing the paradox — they become no more than the product of our fantasies, turned into grotesques, nudes, hybrids. We know they are imaginary beings because, look — we have imagined them! At worst they are the products of an unregulated mind, at gentlest they are child-like companions who teach our children a regard for wayside flowers while allowing them to exercise an appropriate level of imagination. Visualising, though, is also intrinsically dangerous when dealing with such a liminal concept. The process gives shape to whatever it is that we glimpse out of the corner of the eye or disturb in the foliage. When not entirely banal, all representations of fairies have a sinister aspect — they show what so very nearly is, and we always greet it with recognition.

Notes

1. Grimms' *Kinder und Hausmärchen* was first published in 1812, with a second volume appearing in 1814. The English translation by Edgar Taylor appeared in two volumes published 1823 and 1826. Between then and the end of the century the stories appeared in at least thirty different volumes, some featuring new translations, selections, illustrations and re-writings.
2. In 1994, fantasy illustrator, Brian Froud, humorously explored the same connection in *Lady Cottington's Pressed Fairy Book*, under the conceit that a Victorian lady might have gathered, categorised and preserved fairy types in much the same way as she would wild flowers or butterflies.
3. 'Richard Dadd Puck piece from Shakespeare's *A Midsummer Night's Dream* prevails in Preston', *Culture 24* (11 April 2011): http://www.culture24.org.uk/art/painting-and-drawing/art353703 Accessed 19 May 2015.

Part II
Insidious
Intrusions

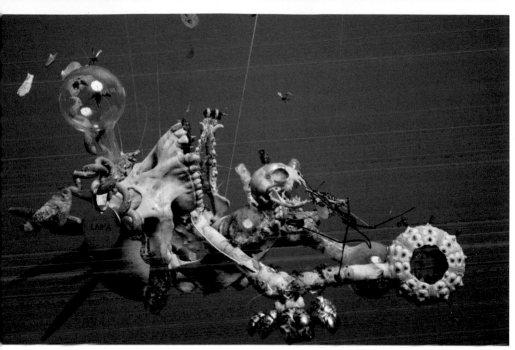

Tessa Farmer, *Cosmic Cloud*, 2012. | Fig 1

Mat Collishaw, *Butterflies and Flowers*, 2005. | Fig 2

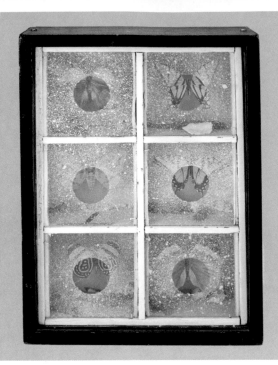

Fig 3 | Joseph Cornell, *Untitled (Butterfly Habitat)*, c.1940.

Fig 4 | Sir Joseph Noel Paton, *The Reconciliation of Oberon and Titania*, 1847.

Fig 5 | Richard Dadd, *The Fairy Feller's Master-Stroke*, 1855–64. →

Fig 6 | Tessa Farmer, *The Horde (detail)*, 2013.

Fig 7 | Tessa Farmer, *A Prize Catch*, 2010.

Tessa Farmer, *The Coming of The Fairies (detail)*, 2011. | Fig 8

Richard Doyle, *Fairy Rings and Toadstools*, 1875. | Fig 9

Fig 10 | Arthur Rackham, *The Kensington Gardens Are in London Where the King Lives*, 1906.

Tessa Farmer, *The Perilous Pursuit of a Python*, 2013. | Fig 11

Fig 12 | Tessa Farmer, *The Depraved Pursuit of a Possum*, 2013.

Film still from *Phase IV*, feature film, directed by Saul Bass, USA, 1974. | Fig 13

Film still from *Phase IV*, feature film, directed by Saul Bass, USA, 1974. | Fig 14

Mark Thompson, *Immersion (Self-Test with Bee Queen)*, performance and film, USA, 1974-76/2012. | Fig 15

Fig 16 | Tessa Farmer, *Cerberus (detail)*, 2008.

Fig 17 | Tessa Farmer, *The Perilous Pursuit of a Python (detail)*, 2013.

Tessa Farmer, *Unwelcome Visitors (detail)*, 2014. | Fig 18

Tessa Farmer, *Unwelcome Visitors (detail)*, 2014. | Fig 19

Fig 20 | Tessa Farmer, *Mignon, ambushed by a mob of fairies (detail)*, 2013.

Fig 21 | Tessa Farmer, *The Hedgehog Host and the Fairy Horde* (detail), 2010.

Fig 22 | Tessa Farmer, *In Fairyland (detail)*, 2015.

So Small, So Fierce, So Hungry

Jeremy Harte

How small do you have to be before you're not really there at all? The Muryans of Cornwall were once part of the world of men and women but, as a consequence of some dreadful forgotten wrong, they were condemned to shrink with each passing generation. Already in the time of Robert Hunt, fifteen decades ago, they seemed about to be lost from the surface of the earth.[1] By now they have become nano-fairies, minute, imperceptible, beyond the reach of memory or imagination.

Fellow-travellers with Faerie get quite indignant about this sort of thing. Somebody, somewhere, must be to blame—perhaps it is the middle classes, or it could be the Disney corporation — for putting about the demeaning idea that fairies are tiny little things. Whereas in the days of old, when folk culture was free and honest and unsentimental, the fairies were a people as robust as any other. They would fight with a man and knock him down; they would steal a woman and have children by her. These were fairies worth taking seriously. 'Can you wonder that the People of the Hills don't care to be confused with that painty-winged, wand-waving, sugar-and-shake-your-head set of imposters?' says Puck of Pook's Hill, and Dan replies 'We don't mean that sort. We hate 'em too'.[2]

Most people with a taste for folklore will agree with Dan and Una, except that it doesn't make much sense to agree with two fictional characters, especially a pair who have just been acting out *A Midsummer Night's Dream*, which is a fiction within a fiction, and have thereby raised Puck, who... No, let's stop there. When it comes to the fairies themselves, we must lull asleep that censor who discriminates between the genuine and the false. There are other, more important things to be said about the secret people. But then, if we are going to abandon our prejudice in favour of the real, the uncontrovertibly authentic folk fairy, then we will have to spend more time thinking seriously about those who are minute, if not necessarily charming.

'According to the description they give who pretend to have seen them, they are in the shape of men, exceeding little.' That sounds rather patronising, doesn't it? 'They dance in moonlight when mortals are asleep and not capable of seeing them, as may be observed on the following morn... For as they dance hand in hand, and so make a circle in their dance, so next day there will be seen rings and circles on the grass.' Pretty, pretty. But this is not some fantasy out of the Victorian nursery. It comes from the wellspring of English folklore studies, the *Antiquitates Vulgares* of the Revd. Henry Bourne, published at Newcastle in 1725. It didn't pay, even then, to disregard a Geordie fairy. 'There are some living who were stolen away by them, and confined seven years'.[3] That is the last, obscure appearance in English lore of the richly detailed mythology of abduction which had once spread through medieval Europe and would still be active more than two hundred years later in the Irish countryside. But, threatening though they could be, these fairies are still authentically tiny.

Bourne was a clergyman, writing not to celebrate folklore but to pin down such aspects of it as needed suppression; so he might seem an unreliable witness. But what about John Clare? Nobody could dispute his knowledge of what ordinary, rural people thought in his native Northamptonshire; nevertheless, in his *Shepherd's Calendar* he writes in the same vein, of how:

> *Tiny things*
> *Will leave their moonlight meadow rings*
> *And unperceived through keyholes creep*
> *When all's in bed and fast asleep*
> *And crowd in cupboards as they please*
> *As thick as mites in rotten cheese*
> *To feast on what the cotter leaves.*[4]

So there was a tradition of miniature fairies which bridged the gap between the oral and the literary. Clare was able to work it up into published poetry because the imagery that he remembered from his childhood was already there to be found in works such as Michael Drayton's *Nymphidia* (1627), in which the elfin knights ride crickets and arm themselves with straws for spears and cockleshells for shields.

Nymphidia is a weak poem not because its fairies are small, but because they are nothing else. The notion of heroic acts on a tiny scale wears thin after 700 lines in which the only thing that matters is the repeated imagination of things being very little. After all, Drayton got his ideas about a fairy realm, as every author did, from *A Midsummer Night's Dream*. And the fairies of the *Dream* do matter, a great deal. Their concord offers good seasons, their dissension brings foul weather, their blessing promises fertility. They can put a girdle round the world, and they treat mortals — those at least who stray into the enchanted wood — as their playthings.

Yes, but how big are they? One obvious answer — they're about the size of the actors who play them — is disallowed by the facts of theatre history. After the close of its initial reception in the 1620s, right through to its veneration by the Romantics, the *Dream* existed only in the study, a physically unrealisable text. William Hazlitt dismissed the idea of actual performance with the put-down that a six-foot fairy would be impossible on stage, and producers and audiences seem to have agreed.[5]

For the supernatural world of the *Dream* is not just a design problem, like the witches in *Macbeth*, to be solved by clever work in the make-up room. It is incapable of any consistent realisation at all. When we enter the court of Titania, we are not looking at the human world scaled down by a model-maker at 1:42. She herself, obviously, is the same size as Bottom. Cobweb and Peaseblossom are smaller, but with a wilfully variable smallness which enables them to shake hands with their mistress' favourite and at the same time to offer him honey-bags stolen from the bees (so are they the same size as bees?) and to feed him apricots, mulberries and figs (so they are able to lift and carry the fruit). Some of this is to be expected of child-actors, and some of it is the consequence of a particular poetical tradition, but no attempt at all is made to co-ordinate the action with the poetry.

Instead, Shakespeare has accepted dream-logic, or rather the logic of storytelling. The first principle here is that things are what they are for the time that attention is focused on them, and no longer. A hero enters the ogre's house; though the ogre is vast and towers over him, he can walk in and sit down at his table. He wins the heart of the ogre's daughter, who finds somewhere for him to hide, and then she prepares her father's supper, cuddles up next to his grim bulk, and extracts the secret of ogreish invulnerability. Now, what size is the daughter? What size is the house? The questions are meaningless because the answer varies according to where our attention is focused at any given time. The 'wee wee man' of the ballad is small, but how small varies on which version of the ballad you are hearing:

> *Thick and short was his legs,*
> *And sma and thin was his thie,*
> *And atween his een a flee might gae,*
> *And atween his shouthers were inches three*

— that sounds fairylike, but in other versions his shoulders are three spans wide (about human size) or three ells (gigantic). No matter: he can hurl a rock that the narrator could scarcely lift, a clear sign of the supernatural, and proceeds to act as his guide to the otherworldly realms.[6]

We are not told who the wee, wee man was; indeed, we aren't even told what he is called, and this is common in Faerie. Shakespeare's

Puck, if you read the stage directions carefully, is actually one puck out of many, distinguished with a by-line as Robin Goodfellow; and even Robin is not a specific name, but a general term for trickster spirits. The tradition-bearers talk loosely of spirits called brownies and buccas, but as soon as we move to the level of the particular narrative, then it is a singular Brownie and Bucca who take centre stage and who are treated as personalities in their own right. Beginning with the general idea of a *bean sí*, a fairy woman, we proceed, as soon as the heart-stopping tale of grief and loss gains pace, to the Banshee. It is all a matter of focus.

And just as fairies often lack fixed names and identities, so they seem — at least in this particular genre of story and memorate — to lack individuality. Whatever they do, they do it all together; whatever happens, happens to them all at once. Consider the curious experience of William Butterfield when he opened up the hillside spa at Ilkley one Midsummer morning in about 1815:

> *All over the well, skimming on its surface like water-spiders, or dipping into it as if they were taking a bath, was a swarm of little people, the biggest of them not above eighteen inches high. They bathed with all their clothes on; and Butterfield noticed that they were dressed from head to foot in green — as green as the colour of grasshoppers. There was such a quantity of them, and they were so agile, and lively, and frolicsome, that he felt he might as soon have tried to catch them as if they had been a swarm of may-flies or a shoal of minnows.*

Once disturbed, they were off, tumbling and bouncing over the wall of the enclosure 'with such a great buzzing and humming, like a swarm of gigantic bluebottle flies, that they quite confused Butterfield's faculties'.[7]

The Ilkley fairies had resented being seen — a universal fairy trait. But they had resisted the gaze not, as others might, through invisibility, but through a kind of hypervisibility, a ubiquity which defeated the senses of their human observer. It is the same strategy as that used by the leprechaun who, promising faithfully not to take the garter off the ragwort clump that marks the hidden gold, fills the field instead with a hundred clumps and a hundred garters: the abundance of detail makes knowledge impossible. For humans should not seek to know too much about fairies. The husband who asks his elfin wife where she goes at night is asking for trouble. The hard-bargaining dwarf or troll in fairy tale, claiming his due unless the heroine can find out his name, seems pretty confident that this won't be general knowledge. Fairies are natural anarchists; they have no intention of being over-ruled by us, and their definition of rule is much the same as Proudhon's — 'to be governed is to be watched, inspected, spied upon, directed, law-driven, numbered, regulated, enrolled, indoctrinated, preached at, controlled, checked, estimated, valued, censured, commanded, by creatures who have neither the right nor the wisdom nor the virtue to do so.' Hardly surprising, then, that human resistance movements have so often gathered under the fairy banner.[8]

And multiplicity, while it may make the individual fairy into something tiny, does not diminish the power of fairies overall. They are a swarm, and just as a swarm of bees is equal in venom and biomass to a large and dangerous creature, so the vengeance of a crowd of fairies is not to be trifled with. Many stories emphasise the helplessness of the human who has broken some fairy rule or taboo, and is assailed by a swirling, intangible cloud of malice.

> *A palm of pins or needles, so small that she didn't notice them, stuck in her fingers... She felt a great number of the small tribe — a score or more — leap on her back, neck, and head. At the same time others, tripping up her heels, laid her flat on the ground.*[9]

These fairies don't strike, they sting. Analogy with insects is obviously present in the storyteller's mind, without in any way diminishing the respect with which the fairies are regarded. And the analogy can work the other way round, as well; insects have been treated as supernatural beings. An Old English verse forcing a swarm of bees to settle opens:

Stay, victorious women, sink to earth!
Never fly wild to the wood.[10]

Well, that makes sense — or does it? The Anglo-Saxons, like everyone else in the ancient world, thought that bees were male, with each hive ruled by a king.[11] The 'victorious women' charm is therefore stealing an image, or a formulaic poetic line, from somewhere else — probably from a charm. 'Mighty women' appear in the magical *Charm Against a Sudden Stitch*, attacking the afflicted man with magical little spears. The attack is described in several ways, one of them being 'shot of elves,' and elfshot continued for many years to function as an explanation for sudden, physically inexplicable pains.[12]

In all this, we are not dealing with firm identities, but with likenesses. The old manuscripts do not say that bees actually are a sort of elves, or that elves themselves are to be equated with those fierce supernatural women who troubled the imagination of the old North. Charm-work, like storytelling, raises images in the mind which are allowed to rise and fall without maintaining a rigorous logical connection. But there is, all the same, a web of analogy which extends from charm to story, from oral to written, and from English to Latin. Then, once we are in the orbit of a much more rigorous Latin-speaking culture, other problems arise: for the medieval Latin equivalent of elf was *demon*.

Now we are heading towards uncomfortable places. Remember how, at that first meeting with the two children, Puck is very careful to put a clear line between himself and other, less agreeable beings. 'I began as I mean to go on. A bowl of porridge, a dish of milk, and a little quiet fun with the country folk in the lanes was enough for me then, as it is now. I belong here, you see, and I have been mixed up with people all my days.'[13] We are in Old England, a realm which absorbs, accepts and assimilates all incomers... but that is no country for religion, whose doctrines insist on division between good and evil.

But likenesses are not so rigid as identities: and we can at least say, without doing violence to traditional ways of thinking, that some of the ways of fairies are very much like the ways of devils. In the queer nooks and corners of demonology, we learn that demons mislead night-wanderers, laughing at their harm; that they have no backs to them, being all hollowed out inside like a mould; that they offer gifts of gold, which in the morning turn out to be dry leaves. Again and again, the motifs that are to become so familiar in fairylore of the eighteenth and nineteenth centuries make their first appearance centuries earlier, in a very different context. Small size, for instance; what are we to make of the demon who was small enough to sit unnoticed on a lettuce-leaf? A girl went in the garden to pick some salad, nibbling as she went, and the silly thing didn't make the sign of the cross before she ate, so she swallowed the demon whole. It took an exorcism to make her better — so says St. Gregory the Great in his *Dialogues*, read and repeated from the sixth century onwards as an authoritative source on the supernatural. Centuries later, another saint laughs quietly as he sees a fine lady turn round and cross the room. Afterwards, in a private conversation, he confesses that he has the gift of seeing devils; that half a dozen of them, sitting on proud madam's trailing dress, were swept off as she turned around; and that the effect was irresistibly funny.

Context is everything. An evil spirit, however awesome and frightening he may be to ordinary sinners, is despised by the saints; in proportion as he is not feared, he becomes smaller, more childish, more comic. Generally speaking, once people have come to some kind of accommodation with spirits, they lose their terror of them, even if they still keep a healthy respect. All the lore that tells you how to deal with fairies — all those instructions not to pry, not to interrupt, to give thanks or keep silence as appropriate, and to be careful when throwing out the washing-water in the evening — they are all reminders that the other lot will abide by rules, just as humans do, even if their rules seem arbitrary. They do not have the motiveless malignancy of the truly bad things. They can be lived with.

And so malice is tempered into mischief. The overwhelming terror of some strange thing smashing into the home is gradually hedged around with traditions and stories in which intruders can be dealt with, if you keep your wits about you. A boy was sitting up late, all on his own before the dying fire, when a lovely little creature jumped down the chimney and stared at him. They exchanged names, as children do; at least, she said that she was called Ainsel, and he cannily said that he was called My Ainsel. For a while they played together like children of one race, but she got hurt and shrieked, and then a voice like thunder rolled down the chimney. 'Who hurt tha?' 'My Ainsel!' 'Well then, tha's the one to blame.' And a hairy hand hauled the adventurous youngling back up the chimney while the little boy cowered in bed.[14]

Here, tradition, instead of making the fairies as small as children, has instead imagined a fairy child, which is not a very common image: most fairies go about their business as adults. By contrast, the changeling — perhaps the most ubiquitous figure in fairy tradition, the one who is remembered when every other story has been forgotten — is a child only in appearance. The tale of the changeling (to roll up all the variations into one) begins with a baby who does not do anything that a good baby should do: doesn't thrive, doesn't fatten, doesn't sleep, but is simply ravenous for food and attention. And slowly, as suspicion dawns that something is not right, the mother turns to some timeworn formula for testing the little stranger — doing her brewing in eggshells, say — and the elf reveals that he is in fact a wizened old creature who has been freeloading under the guise of a baby.[15]

There is a curious tension here between two understandings of what a changeling might be. At the beginning of the story, the implied logic is that fairies want to exchange their children for ours. At the denouement, we have shifted to the quite different idea that fairies who are already adult — beyond adult, in fact; forbiddingly, millennially old — will steal our food and affection by playing the part of a child. You can't make sense of these two images in a single framework; in fact, you can't make much sense of either of them separately. What's the attraction for an elf — even a hypergeriatric elf — of lying around in a cradle all day?

Tradition does not ask these questions, because tradition is dealing with the living image as it arises through the story, not assembling logical explanations. And so what matters about the changeling, as the story works its way from the opening problem to the final resolution, is not whether he is infant or elderly or antediluvian, but that he is hungry. The intolerable strains inflicted by the otherworldly stranger on the human householder are summed up by his appropriation of the nourishment that belongs to a human baby: except that unlike a baby, he does not make any return in growth or affection. Getting food, and giving nothing for it, breaks the core bond of human sociability.

At the conclusion of the changeling story everything is set right: the fairy stranger is evicted from the human home and the bonds of nurture are reasserted with the return of the rightful baby. Expulsion and return intersect at the gaping mouth of the chimney, which in a traditional household acts as the focal point of cooking, but which is also an opening from hearth and home into the outside world; one which, obviously and practically, cannot be shut and barred in the way that doors and windows can. This is the place where the housewife carries out her brewery in eggshells, a form of deliberate anti-cooking. This is also the location at which, in the more brutal conclusions to the changeling story, the unwanted stranger is placed on a shovel as if to be cooked on the hot coals — until the elf recognises that the game is up, and bounds up shrieking and laughing through the chimney-hole.

That is a two-way traffic, though, for unwanted things can come down the chimney as well as up, like the little stranger in the Ainsel story; and though tradition has furnished a wealth of protective devices — pins, charms, scythe blades, branches of rowan — which can be used to defend that gap, it's still physically there. It is a passage as necessary to the home as orifices are to the human body, and like them it cannot be sealed literally, but only through the work of culture.

The exclusion was imperfect, as you might expect in a traditional house, never very effectively proofed against the outside world. Warped wood, rotten thatch and weathered daub let in little creatures as readily as they did wind and rain. Clare's fairies, who 'crowd in cupboards... to feast on what the cotter leaves', are behaving just like ants or mice. Two centuries earlier, Robert Kirk spoke of them:

preying on the grain as do Crows and Mice... their robberies ...
oftimes occasione great Ricks of corn not to bleed so well (as they
call it) or prove so copious by verie far as was expected by the
owner.[16]

Kirk hesitates to say that the thefts of the fairies are actual, physical appropriations — which is inevitable given that his philosophy, or physics, or whatever it is, postulates a middle status for these creatures of congealed air. They are not solid matter like us, but they are not spirits like angels, either. And therefore their food is not literal grains of wheat, nor is it a purely metaphorical image; it is, instead, 'the foyson or substance of cornes and liquors' which (one gathers) can still apparently remain on the pantry shelf as solid-looking as they were before, but with their inner nourishing substance subtly taken away. The food continues to look like food, just as the changeling looks like a baby, but behind the external appearances there is something lacking.

Food was scarce and hard-won in the peasant communities of the past, so why should they have been so ready to imagine it being appropriated by these light-fingered strangers? Mice are bad enough, but we don't really have an option not to believe in mice, whereas fairies seem more like a matter of opinion. But subjecting tradition to rational interrogations of this sort vastly overestimates how much freedom anybody ever has to imagine or not imagine what they will about the world. When it comes to food, for instance, the wants and powers of fairies are only part of much wider patterns of thought — patterns which arise from the most basic issues of subsistence.

For a peasant household, supplying its own wants as best as it can, food makes two demands on the workforce: it has to be grown, and it has to be preserved. Corn is ground into flour and baked as bread, barley is malted and brewed into beer, milk is churned into butter and cheese. In each case a series of transformations is needed to turn perishable raw stuff into durable provisions which can be stacked in larder or cellar as a protection against hungry times. And like any transformation of raw nature, these kitchen operations come to stand more generally for culture itself.

Now, the fairies are neither human nor animal, and that is reflected in their diet. They do not hunt or graze on wild food, but they don't seem to grow their own either; instead, they benefit at one remove from people's labour, and then they have a preference for the distinctly human creations of bread, butter and beer. Often they pre-empt supplies of food at the moment of transformation itself, and as the fairy in the *Dream* says of Puck:

> *Bootless make the breathless housewife churn,*
> *And sometimes make the drink to bear no barm.*

You could make a functional explanation out of this, remembering that processes which involve yeast, rennet, gels, pickles and other agents of fermentation and transformation are all notoriously unreliable, and that until recently their biochemistry was a mystery. When things went wrong, it could be blamed on the foyson being taken by fairies, and that made everyone feel better: nothing is more vexing to the imagination than misfortune without a cause. On the other hand, while fairy theft was perhaps a sufficient explanation for butter that didn't come or dough that wouldn't rise, it wasn't one which was necessary. Other agents of misfortune, from sin to witches, could be invoked, and often were. People were convinced that the fairies stole human food, not because they needed an explanation of why fermentation and similar processes went wrong, but because they had a particular idea of the supernatural which only the fairy tradition could satisfy.

Theft seems an odd foundation for relations between this world and the other; it implies an unexpected combination of dependence with power. Gods, I suppose, can demand that we give them things; monsters can take; the dead can beg; but it is only an elfin race that can be expected to pilfer from us.

At the heart of Faerie, many of these traditions suggest, was a lack which could only be supplied by human things. It is as if they had a less substantial life, one which could only have been sustained with a flow of food, goods, even people, from our world to theirs. You can see this, if you like, as a metaphor for the continued work of fantasy which sustained those golden dwellings on the other side. Or perhaps it was the fairies who exacted, over so many centuries, such a continual tribute of the imagination.

We blink; the enchanted vision flits. In a few short generations, the company of fairies, which had once been as indisputably present as the warmth of sun and the breath of wind and the eye of God, is gone. Gone from belief, but not necessarily from culture — for art, as the more high-minded Victorians insisted, can be brought in to supply the place of faith. Tessa Farmer's fairies, with their vividly imagined vindictive lives, their swarming struggles just outside the reach of human perception — these are traditional fairies in everything but their materiality; and that, too, has been crafted so deftly small as to be almost invisible. Who would be surprised if, on the eve of her next gallery exhibition, the suspended frameworks and intricate mounts should suddenly become empty, and only a fierce shrill laughter fill the air?

Notes

1. Robert Hunt, *Popular Romances of the West of England* (London: John Camden Hotten, 1865), 1: 65.
2. Rudyard Kipling, *Puck of Pook's Hill* (London: Macmillan, 1906), 14.
3. Henry Bourne, *Antiquitates Vulgares* (Newcastle upon Tyne: Privately, 1725), 82.
4. John Clare, *The Shepherd's Calendar*, edited by Eric Robinson and David Powell (Oxford University Press, 1993), January lines 121–6.
5. Beatrice Phillpotts, *Fairy Paintings* (London: Ash and Grant, 1978), 7.
6. Francis James Child, *The English and Scottish Popular Ballads* (Boston: Houghton Mifflin, 1882–98), 2:329–34.
7. Simon Young, 'Three Notes on West Yorkshire Fairies in the Nineteenth Century', *Folklore* 123: 223–30 at 225–6.
8. Andy Letcher, 'The Scouring of the Shire: Fairies, Trolls and Pixies in Eco-protest Culture', *Folklore* 112 (2001): 147–61.
9. William Bottrell, *Traditions and Hearthside Stories of West Cornwall* (Penzance: Bottrell, 1879–8), 2: 163.
10. Godfrid Storms, *Anglo-Saxon Magic* (The Hague: Martinus Nijhoff, 1948), 137.
11. T.H. White, *The Book of Beasts* (London: Jonathan Cape, 1954), 154–5.

12. Karen Louise Jolly, *Popular Religion in Late Saxon England* (University of North Carolina Press, 1996), 137–40.

13. Kipling, 15.

14. M.A. Richardson, *The Local Historian's Table Book, of... Newcastle-on-Tyne, Northumberland and Durham* (London: J.R. Smith, 1843–6), B1: 325.

15. Séamas Mac Philib, 'The Changeling (ML5085): Irish Versions of a Migratory Legend in their International Context', *Béaloideas* 59 (1991): 121–31.

16. Michael Hunter, *The Occult Laboratory: Magic, Science and Second Sight in Late Seventeenth-Century Scotland* (Woodbridge: Boydell, 2001), 79.

Swarming Fever: Tessa Farmer's Evil Evolution

Petra Lange-Berndt

Once upon a time, around 1900 in Pitt Street, Kensington, there was a young woman called Miss Vulliamy running a dainty little shop. She was known for her unfeminine 'new art', making, as a journalist describes it, vases and grotesque 'puck, pogg, and pixie pots [...] in the form of goblins' faces, malignant or benign; in the form of inanely-smiling frogs, of bats with nightmare jaws and wings, of ultra-owlish owls, and of fish and fowl'.[1] But above all, as this report in a popular magazine tells us, Miss Vulliamy was famous for 'Beautifying Bones': in her studio, that resembled a medical museum, she had discovered the secret of transforming bodily remains into objects of exquisite yet nightmarish craftsmanship such as vases made out of clay and china resembling a long-eared demon, 'angels in flight' or 'a creature of the centipede type'.[2]

Despite an abundance of such practices, the art history of this field that mixes outsider and applied art with what feminist Lucy Lippard had coined 'Making Something from Nothing' and the methods and materials of the medical and natural history museum is still only emerging.[3] Tessa Farmer's creations clearly belong in this context, consisting largely of natural materials assembled with super-glue.

One is presented, for instance, with the dried exoskeletons of animals — social insects such as ants, bees, wasps or hornets and another group of arthropods, crustaceans with their spikes and claws. But Farmer, who in 2007 had a residency at the Natural History Museum, London, is not only interested in entomology but also in dreams, myths and poetry. Around 2000 the first fairy was born, spotted by the artist in a vibrant red tulip; others spontaneously emerged from trees and shrubs. But we are not meeting a variant of the *Flower Fairies*, which the English illustrator, Cicely Mary Barker, made popular in the first half of the twentieth century, usually depicting well-behaved children or polite adolescents. Farmer calls her fairies affectionately *Little Savages* but at the same time lets the distinction between wild and cultivated collapse.[4] Her skeletal, winged and strangely sexless creatures undermine clear distinctions between the worlds of the living and the dead when they resonate with hell, where Beelzebub is the lord of the flies and forms lose their integrity.[5] They have ancestors in the fallen angels that resulted from the War in Heaven or those who torture poor souls in depictions of the Last Judgement.[6]

But while it was reported that Miss Vulliamy's creatures 'never swarm nor flew anywhere but in fairy books [...]'[7] the art of Tessa Farmer is of a completely different order — her mischievous creatures, that are linked to buzzing and skirring insects and their behaviour, quickly adapted to their surroundings and shrank. By now they are tiny, almost invisible, and easily slip under the radar of human perception. They live their lives almost in secret. And they are by no means fair. As Farmer informs us in her stories that are scattered throughout interviews, catalogues and press releases, her installations cannot be connected to ideas of a paradisiacal nature. Instead, goblins prey on fairies and fairies in turn 'feed on ants and other insects, and steal wood ant larvae to spin protective cocoons for their young whilst they are growing'.[8] The hybrid life forms which the artist is observing in order to survive constantly enslave or fight animals that appear within a compound, a network, colony or swarm (Fig A). What is Farmer fiddling with, creating these creepy clusters?

In German the verb 'to swarm' — *schwärmen* — has multiple meanings. It points to the specific behaviour of insects but also suggests the idea of getting excited about something while losing touch with reality; the *Schwärmer* becomes an ecstatic daydreamer.[9] But I do not want to go down this route of creating binaries of fact and fancy, actual and fictitious. Farmer strongly insists on her belief in fairies; that they are perfectly real for her. But which reality is at stake here? To follow some of the tales told by philosophers Gilles Deleuze and Félix Guattari in their *Thousand Plateaus*, the question is not: is it true, but: does it work? What new thoughts does this art practice enable, what actions to carry out? What new emotions does it make possible? What sensations and perceptions does it enable?[10]

The Age of Insects

Even though Farmer engages in the art of micro-bricolage linked to the world of the miniature, her installations do not invite the magnifying gaze of the microscope, usually resulting in a double pinning down of the creature under consideration — actual and within a visual regime.[11] Her immersive installations, that partly escape photographic representation, enable the reverse when, after zooming in to the details of a butterfly or bee, one suddenly becomes aware of an even smaller body, torturing the former, and, in turn, of an unknown world: The human eye with its prosthetic lenses is reminded of its limits. Nevertheless, similarly to the Mexican *Dressed Fleas* from 1905 that one can encounter at the Natural History Museum at Tring (Fig B), the nearly invisible can create increased attention. According to literary critic and poet Susan Stewart it is 'emblematic of craft and discipline; while the materiality of the product is diminished, the labour involved multiplies, and so does the significance of the total object'.[12] The miniature becomes a stage on which we project, on which we imagine that the

> world of things can open itself to reveal a secret life — indeed,
> to reveal a set of actions and hence a narrativity and history
> outside the given field of perception [...].[13]

Petra Lange-Berndt

Since we are looking at social animals — and social fairies — one could argue that rather than emphasising a skilful and godlike maker or triggering escapist daydreams, in the art of Tessa Farmer this process continually points outside itself. For example, in installations such as *The Horde* (2013) where, due to the elaborate exhibition architecture, the borders between the habitats of human, fairy and insect merge, our attention is drawn to the entanglement of the assembled creatures with their surroundings — and to us.[14] An insect colony always pulverises and overflows space, spreading, pouring, and invading. Many entomologists considered social insects with the mixture of admiration and horror that we might display towards Farmer's creatures; these animals clearly let humans create a diversity of tales. According to poet and beekeeper Maurice Maeterlinck, for instance, in the world of insects 'the marvellous and the unexpected confront us so constantly — occurring far more frequently [...] than in the most miraculous fairy stories [...]'.[15] Farmer's art enables these affects — spheres of experiences that fall outside of the dominant paradigm of representation — in that she lets one 'believe in the existence of a very special becoming-animal traversing human beings and sweeping them away, affecting the animal no less than the human'.[16]

It is the introduction of the *objets trouvès* of the hollow, dried-out bodies of animals and, mostly, of insects that enables this important shift from the nostalgic dollhouse to ecology.[17] While the cultural product of the miniature normally assumes an anthropocentric universe for its absolute sense of scale,[18] the fairies are actually modelled in relation to the bodies of their preserved *insect* counterparts. And civilisations of social insects precede the appearance of humankind on our planet by at least a hundred million years; ants, for instance, survive from the Jurassic age of dinosaurs. As we all have experienced, these organisms are everywhere, even in an urban environment; flies buzzing around, spiders in corners and cockroaches under the kitchen sink.

← Fig A Tessa Farmer, *The Hunt*, detail: *Fairy Throwing Ants from a Cicada*, 2011, bones, insects, plant roots, hedgehog spines, exhibition *Minimal*, Hå Gamle Prestegard, Nærbø, Norway 2012.

Fig B Fleas dressed as dancers by a Mexican woman, 1905,
Natural History Museum at Tring.

They cannot be anthropomorphised as easily and largely live outside
of cultivated natural zones such as zoos, or farms and human homes.
They are the unfamiliar animal, the definitive organisms of *différance*.[19]
The 1990s saw at least two installations where thousands of insects
were killed — Damien Hirst's *A Thousand Years* (1992) and Mark
Dion's *The Great Munich Bug Hunt* (1993) — and nobody protested.
As writer Elias Canetti phrased it: 'Their blood does not stain our
hands, for it does not remind us of our own'.[20] At the same time,
insects play the central role for the ecological equilibrium as well as
the diversity of species and we would know very little about human
genetics without the laboratory animal of the fruit fly. It seems as if
'the reign of birds [...] has been replaced by the age of insects, with its
much more molecular vibrations, chirring, rustling, buzzing, clicking,
scratching, and scraping'.[21] Dion has been very conscious of this
when he writes: 'Insects constitute the absolute majority of the fauna
of this planet. Actually we do not live in the age of animals, but in the
age of insects'.[22]

Keeping this in mind, it is ever more surprising to realise that insects have been marginalised as the subjects of art production.[23] For a long time they were the footnotes of pictorial narrations, only to emerge as main actors in subgenres such as the slippery habitats of the gloomy seventeenth century *sotto bosco*, the life in the undergrowth, inhabited by poisonous-looking plants, snakes, toads, and moths; a related field is the accurate etymological illustrations of Maria Sibylla Merian and her followers. But most of these artists were interested in finding beauty in nature, meaning searching for a likeness to what had been defined as the human form. Farmer's swarms and hordes, on the contrary, are deeply unsettling because they are disrupting this order. In complex installations such as *The Fairy Horde and the Hedgehog Host* (2010; Fig 21: see colour insert) sadistic fairies employ hedgehog spine spears, sea urchin spine clubs and the stings of captive wasps to kill; on other occasions they install the silken nets of captive spiders or use earwigs as weapons in order to fight with their arch-enemies, the wasps.[24] For instance, in *A Prize Catch* (2009; Fig 7: see colour insert), fairies, like insects, keep death alive when they break down corpses, 'stealing and remodelling the flesh, causing the desired unity and wholeness of the body to fragment, erode, and threaten ultimately to disappear completely'.[25] And this behaviour is not unusual in the world of beetles and butterflies. Within entomological narrations one finds ants, which have been the 'immemorial enemy'[26] of termites for the 'past two or three millions of years',[27] spraying formic acid. One also comes across termite soldiers carrying syringes; there are the 'great honey thief, the huge *Sphinx atropos*, the sinister moth that bears a death's head on its back'[28] and parasites on the watch for opportunities of plunder. Insects thematise a concept of nature that is not about peace and harmony but about the change from a static to a dynamic concept of the world. They point to the chaotic struggle of life as it was increasingly discussed in evolutionary theories emerging from the early nineteenth century onwards. The once-clear distinction between animal and human became blurred, unstable, and even obsolete in this 'web of complex relations' as Darwin famously describes it in 1859.[29] Unlike nature as conceived by the Greeks, the Enlightenment and the rationalist Christian tradition, this model of nature held no clues for human conduct, no answers to moral dilemmas: 'Pitiless cruelty, torment, and destruction of the weak and innocent. The thief, the assassin, the bloodstained robber, these are her [nature's] favourites, these are the [...] triumphant victors of the strife'.[30] Nature became the product of chance and humans nothing more than an intelligent mutation. The tales of selection, variation, destruction and extinction were quickly popularised and this upheaval triggered anxieties around race and gender. It was hard enough to imagine that we might be related to apes, but the fear of being close to Darwin's beloved barnacle or an unfamiliar, abject beetle, as it was described by Richard Marsh in *The Beetle* (1897) or Franz Kafka in his famous novel *The Metamorphosis* (1915), was clearly horrifying.

The idea that bodies were becoming plastic was played out to the extreme within the tales of folklore and literature. Farmer grew up with this specific, British brew and it might help to read some of the stories her great-grandfather, Arthur Machen, an orthodox Anglo-Catholic, wrote around the time when Miss Vulliamy was working. He was among the first to create a sense of horror with roots in biology rather than in spirituality.[31] 'The Novel of the Black Seal' (1896), for instance, tells the story of Professor Gregg, an ethnologist who has discovered the existence of a lost race of the hills close to 'brute beasts' that 'had fallen out of the grand march of evolution'.[32] These 'non-Aryan' Little People dwelling beneath ground, in hillocks, are far down the evolutionary tree,[33] associated with regression, mental illness and above all unspeakable evil, the 'chill of death' and demonic powers.[34] More precisely, they guard the horrifying secret of how 'man can be reduced to the slime from which he came, and be forced to put on the flesh of the reptile and the snake'.[35] These beings are shapeshifters themselves occupying an unstable position within evolution, and, indeed, one can repeatedly spot fairies in Farmer's work that, like the zombies in the Chapman Brother's model *Hell* (2000), display spontaneous mutations, for instance, swimfins or a wasp body (Fig 8: see colour insert).[36] Actually, Machen's Little People are connected to the traditions of the Welsh fairies, the *Tylwydd Têg*.[37] As fairy scholar Carole G. Silver explains:

> *At their worst they were simultaneously anarchic, spoiling and ruining the products of human culture, and parasitic, living off their hosts while they destroyed them. What made the fairies especially dangerous was their need of human energy and of human beings [...] They were the folkloric equivalent to the mob or demons, invading the civilized world from the barbaric wilderness [...].*[38]

If Farmer's crazed fairies are mixed into the evolutionary chaos, if they are connected to us, are they the missing link between the human and the insect worlds? Are they early homunculi, fighting for their ecological niche, trying to separate from their insect origins? Or are they antihuman? Do they stand for unsuppressed instinct and violence, the vestiges of the animalistic present in *Homo sapiens*? Is it suggested that a specific condition of the material body results in savage behaviour? Are these fairies actually in line with ideas of social Darwinism pointing to the moment when nature was re-moralised in the name of progress, racialism and nationalism?

Let me try another tale. Deleuze and Guattari have reinterpreted Ernst Haeckel's hierarchical, linear concept of the evolutionary tree of life (Fig C). From their point of view, there is no hidden principle in nature, instead, the 'plan[e] is infinite, you can start it in a thousand different ways [...].'[39] Farmer's art, from this angle, is rather resonating with Arthur Rackham's image *The Kensington Gardens Are in London Where the King Lives* (1906) that transforms the arborescent conception of knowledge into a proliferating field of mischievous wooden gnomes and fairies (Fig 10: see colour insert). The creatures' intentions stay a secret, they cannot be discovered but their actions enable the metamorphosis of things and subjects. It cannot be a coincidence that the bodies of Farmer's fairies are made out of dried rhizomatic plant roots that the artist obtains from her mother's garden. Her hordes of fairies and insects, assembled with so much wit and humour, create

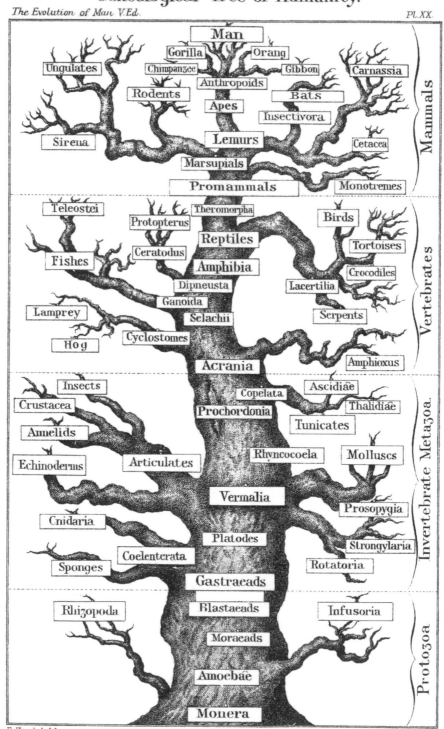

E. Haeckel del.

no unity, not a singular defined individual, but rather a network becoming or embodying different identities with their multiple, heterogeneous perspectives. What is the bumblebee dreaming? What kind of jokes are these grinning fairies telling each other? What is the ant plotting? Fairies upset the known order of things. They resonate with witches who, according to anthropologist Mary Douglas, 'are social equivalents of beetles and spiders who live in the cracks of the walls and wainscoting' because they dwell in the interstices of power structures and therefore can be considered a threat to those whose status is more defined.[40] But toward 'what void does the witch's broom lead?'[41] Rather than evolution by descent and filiation, Farmer's cunning craft obviously concerns symbiosis and alliance.

Fairies in Revolt

The naturalist Carl Linné (Linnaeus) lamented in 1735, in his *Systema naturae*, that, as far as 'the insects are concerned, no one has gone to the trouble of placing them into any kind of order [...]'[42] These animals resist classification; until today scientific measurements include only the length of the body, since considering the many different positions of fragile feelers and spidery legs would produce great confusion. Already, from this angle, insects, famous for their ability to metamorphose, demonstrate a constant state of change. And the epitome of a constantly moving body — as well as a counter-model to Machen's pessimistic concept of deadly primeval slime — is the compound of the social insect, especially the swarm (Fig 6: see colour insert).[43] At the turn of the century, within the entomological discourse on solitary insects, one could find in Jean-Henri Fabre's writings or in the caricatures of social critic Jean Ignace Isidore Gérard (also known as Grandville), a shift in focus to creatures of the crowd such as ants, 'mistresses of the soil,' bees, wasps, who 'rule the air' with their facetted eyes, or photophobic

← Fig C Ernst Haeckel, *Genealogical Tree of Humanity*, lithograph,
originally published in *Anthropogenie oder Entwicklungsgeschichte des Menschen* [...], Leipzig, 1874.

termites.[44] As praised by Russian anarchist, Peter Kropotkin, or Japanese ecologist and anthropologist Imanishi Kinji, social insects have been perfecting mutual aid — the art of self-organisation by co-operative communication, division of labour, and acting together as a functional whole — for eons, beating individual animals in competition for resources.[45] Farmer's fairies with their honeybee wings fight or enslave these social insects, keep them as pets and transport or form mutualistic symbioses with them. Therefore, it is important to understand some basic principles of their behaviour. What literary scholar Claire Preston writes holds true for any social insect: 'One bee is no bee, so almost none of the standard western ideas of individuality and autonomy of self have any purchase in the study of bees. [...] Bees are always communal, plural, public, unindividuated, corporate, en masse'.[46] Colonial animals are for instance masters of sophisticated communication via dance or chemical signals.[47] They display behaviour that has been described as bordering on the supernatural, something that is 'far beyond all our senses [...],'[48] some termites and ants culture fungi in their nests. Moreover, being around almost from the very beginnings of life on earth, these multitudes had made the shift from a hunter-gatherer existence to agriculture long before the evolution of *Homo sapiens*. They even have air-conditioning in their, at times, subterranean nests and employ a celestial compass system when returning from a foraging excursion.[49] As the sensible Maeterlinck writes 'indeed there can be no doubt that [...] the termite knows more than we do [...].'[50]

Even though social insects have been used to discuss the most diverse human societies,[51] in the end this mysterious mass is 'corresponding to senses and properties of matter that are wholly unknown to us [...].'[52] The great majority of the nest-mates are female, born of a queen that is equipped with a spermatheca, an internal 'sperm bank' ripped from the body of her lover during the nuptial flight 'that will render her almost an hermaphrodite'.[53] But, clearly, human terminology is coming to its limits here. I should rather start to chirr, buzz, click, smell, or dance. Clearly, we 'are reminded again of the fairy godmother who waves her wand [...].'[54] Entomologist William Morton Wheeler acted according to these feelings of difference when he displayed an early sensibility towards such non-humans, trying to operate with adapted metaphors that avoid obvious anthropomorphisms: '[...] the animal colony is a true organism and not merely the analogue of the person'.[55] What kind of tales are these 'composite animals',[56] these superorganisms, telling us? Or, rather, smelling? And what does this mean for Farmer's fairies? Where do they live? So far they seem to be nomadic, found on spaceships and other floating devices made out of mice skulls or osseous stuff, powered by enslaved butterflies, beetles and bees. How are they organising themselves, how are they communicating? Are they a matriarchy? Do they have a queen? How do they multiply? What is certain is that Farmer's fairies despise rules. They seem to have left the structure that would bind them to one place, the nest, enabling them to appear everywhere. They are anarchic and in constant revolt, similar to cells that separated themselves from the unifying organism. They are the organs without body, the deserting angels.[57]

It is important that Farmer's fairies appear in swarms.[58] In *Untitled (Hornet Panel)* (2011) artist Alastair Mackie pinned down the heads of hornets on a monochrome black plane so that one is confronted with a phalanx of heads determined to battle. Similar to Hirst, with his pickled fish and farm animals, Mackie is domesticating the demonic power of social animals by submitting them to the logic of geometry and minimalism.[59] His dressed animals are caught within the regime of the clearly-defined picture plane, missing the point that insects cannot be domesticated like cattle; they are truly wild animals. On the contrary, the amateur entomologist and folklorist Farmer arranges her dried-out bodies hovering in mid-air on almost invisible threads, used by magicians for their tricks, according to the behaviour the untameable animals displayed when they were alive. This is a brave move; the unleashed swarm of bees or the seething mass of ants has quite a negative reputation when, actually, the animal compound is at its most vulnerable.[60] Swarms have, for instance, been connected to migration and looting hordes,[61] especially in North America, where one can find numerous disaster films and B-Movies that stage swarms and ant colonies as threat to humankind in its formation as nuclear family or nation state.[62] In this context the contact with these animals is not a liberation but can only result in death. But this is not quite what Farmer has in mind. As Hugh Raffles has been pointing out, insects are everywhere, they eat our food and share our beds. They are also constantly travelling unseen through the seemingly clear blue sky, which should therefore be redefined as 'insect-laden air' from which falls 'a continuous rain':

> *What happens to the notion of an invasive species in the face of this continuous and irrepressible traffic of short- and long-range travel, dispersal, and migration? What is left of a notion that everything has its own place, that everything belongs somewhere and nowhere else, that boundaries are inviolable, that with vigilance and chemicals this hyperabundance of wilful and random life can be brought under control?*[63]

In this spirit, Farmer is avoiding clear definitions that would enable the formation of hierarchies, to classify and to pin down. She has made a pact with demonic fairies which oscillate between human, animal, and mythical creatures, creating affects, in those who spot them. These hordes are continuously expanding, forming 'a multiplicity, a becoming, a population, a tale [...]',[64] occupying spaces both physical and psychological.

The Next Phase

Charlotte Sleigh claims that, for the founder of analytical psychology, Carl Jung, as for many others, the unconscious was an insect.[65] But what happens if Freud's waxen *Wunderblock*, the psychological apparatus,[66] starts to become a multiplicity? A swarm consisting of social insects and fairies? Even though Deleuze and Guattari mainly debate vampires, sorcerers and werewolves, casually they also mention ants and a swarm of mosquitoes.[67] 'Becoming-insect' is definitively a possibility for the two Kafka-scholars to redefine racist models of evolution and their hierarchies. According to Maeterlinck, in the case of bees the anticipation of swarming generates a sense of ecstasy. Bees 'seem bewitched [...] like a living jelly stirred by an invisible hand', while the temperature within the hive is rising to such a degree at times that 'the wax of the buildings will soften, and twist out of shape'.[68] This is clearly a feverish action, erasing memory and destroying any kind of order.[69] And fittingly, the swarming under consideration is actually dedicated to 'the hostile madness of love', 'the most fairy-like that can be conceived, azure and tragic'.[70] The queen bee is mating with one male bee during her flight, but the drone dies immediately after copulation, while all other males will be murdered shortly afterwards. Are Farmer's fairies ultra-radical amazons? But above all, what we witness during the sensual experience of installations such as *The Horde*, where one can get lost in the battle of numerous swarms, is not simply swarming, the reproduction of the colony, but what beekeepers call swarming fever, when more than one swarm is leaving the colony. As in films such as *Empire of the Ants* (USA 1977), pollution and nuclear disasters have led to nature in revolt. Molecular changes launch mutations within the insect world and an uncanny vitality. But most importantly as Deleuze and Guattari have observed in the case of hordes of vampires or packs of werewolves — and the same holds true for fairies — Farmer's swarms infect.[71] According to the artist's tales her little savages are parasites, just like their Victorian ancestors. They seem to have learned a lot from parasitic wasps, which, as entomologist Gavin R. Broad informs us, despite their enormous variety have stayed a 'fantastically obscure group to the public at large'.[72] The female wasp lays eggs on or in the body of other insects; this host is killed when these eggs hatch and serves as food resource. The wasp may eat its way out of the body or remain in the more or less empty skin in order to spin a cocoon. But as if this would not be enough cruel behaviour, some of these wasps have entered into co-operations with viruses that weaken their prey's immune defences and brainwash the unfortunate host to bring about modifications in the receiver advantageous to the egg's development. The fairies have studied this technique closely. As visitors could learn in Farmer's *The Coming of the Fairies* (2011), an installation featuring a swan-ship, 'parasitic fairies laid their eggs into the corners of the bird's eyes, and the larvae burrowed into its brain, eating non-essential tissue, until metamorphosing into adult fairies and taking control of this powerful flying machine'.[73] According to Michel

Serres, the parasite is an insidious infection that weakens without killing, invisible by becoming very small, 'seldom if ever larger than the size of an insect'.[74] The parasite is the unwanted guest but — resulting from multiple meanings of the word in French — also the static in a system or the interference in a channel, 'an interruption, a corruption, a rupture of information [...] who produces disorder and who generates a different order'.[75] The fairies take their meal from the larder of the host's flesh but in return they pay for it with stories.[76] The parasite is a 'little troublemaker',[77] a thermal exciter, causing fever, motion, or paralysis by

> *despoiling actions, like ascaris worms or leeches; by toxic actions, like ticks or fleas; by trauma, like bilharzia or trichina worms; by infection, like dysenteric amoebas; by obstruction, like the filariasis of elephantiasis; by compression, like those that form cysts; by irritations, inflammations, itching; by rashes [...].*[78]

Parasites produce 'slips of the tongue and mispronunciations', 'chaos, noise, disorder. The base of existence.'[79] And most importantly, as Serres reminds us, in our efforts to exclude parasitic phenomena, they are made a part of our every interaction.

Therefore, the swarming activity of Farmer's fairies should also be understood at a conceptual level, as whizzing and whooshing, as a world that consists not of things alone but of passages, something that indicates the swarm intelligence of decentralised, self-organised systems, collective consciousness, communicating in secret, conspiracies and plotting. Swarms disrupt the scientific processes of objectification by means of their dynamics in space and time; they are fuzzy objects like dust, clouds, or fire.[80] In this respect the fairies learned a great deal from the one social insect with whom they have not a hostile but a symbiotic relationship: gangs of ants.[81] The film *Phase IV*, directed by Saul Bass in 1974 during the Cold War, tells us how these animals operate secretly and out of sight. A strange planetary constellation has changed the microstructures of the universe — on planet Earth all ant species have joined forces, taking over the world

Petra Lange-Berndt

in a silent revolution (Fig 13: see colour insert). They have become the matrix of a new world order, undermining the elaborate computer-based technology of the scientists who are chasing them. The ants are forming an uncanny and intelligent network, that, quite different from the swarm metaphors of an engineered present, can neither be decoded nor controlled (Fig 14: see colour insert).

These insects are by no means peaceful, they demand that humans adapt to their lifestyle and revise evolutionary hierarchies. Like the anomal, a demonic swarm member of special lure that peoples Deleuze and Guattari's tales, Saul Bass' ants enable a passage.[82] And Farmer's fairies very much have the same function; clear separations between the sexes or between human and animal have come to an end. Rather, an alliance of different species is proclaimed, as one can spot in the performance and film project *Immersion (Self-Test with Bee Queen)* (USA 1974–76/2012) by artist Mark Thompson (Fig 15: see colour insert).[83] The apiarist-artist abolished the hierarchy of Haeckel's tree of life and became a member of the vibrating compound with its anonymous members. A meditatively buzzing swarm reminiscent of a 'sub atomic level where everything becomes very fluid is replacing the traditional portrait, and Thompson allows himself to 'flow and to melt into these creatures' becoming 'one animal among many'.[84] The artist is not a distanced, shepherd-like beekeeper-father since swarming, after all, is about copulation.[85] He is embracing the possibility of participatory art that involve non-humans and a sexuality that runs contra to conventions. This alliance is not necessarily pleasant or advantageous to the human participants. As Farmer tells us, for the fairies we

> are the ultimate prize and they want to take over the world [...]. It feels a bit like I have been parasitised and they have taken over my brain and they are making me produce them and, you know, at some point all that will be left is a dry husk of me [...] (laughs).[86]

It is not we as visitors who are controlling the micro-worlds of Farmer's installations. As in *Phase IV*, Farmer as well as her audience is part of the whole experimental setting — and in the end the main object of enquiry. Our bodies are filled with signals, noises, messages, and parasites; we are speaking plurivocally, parasites multiply until they reach the level of thunder and fury, producing toxins, inflammations, and fever.[87] Due to the alteration of genes and new experimental cultures in the Anthropocene, human evolution is probably entering a new phase, a phase that Darwin could not have dreamed of. As Donna Haraway has frequently discussed, this does not necessarily mean that we will witness the advent of the superhuman since, at the same time, the problematic concept of the 'pure' *Homo sapiens* is coming to an end.[88] Social insects have been mastering genetic transformations — termites and bees, for instance, mysteriously can transform their offspring either into an ordinary larva or into a queen.[89] Farmer's fairies are clearly interested in such bodily modifications since they have built several labs for experiments; *Cosmic Cloud* (2012) even went into outer space (Fig 1: see colour insert). Instead of genetic localisation and unambiguity, Farmer's art is promising a possible fluidity of bodies and their concepts, the displacement of molecules and the insectoid power of metamorphosis.

> *The parasite doesn't stop. It doesn't stop eating or drinking or yelling or burping or making thousands of noises or filling space with its swarming and din. The parasite is an expansion; it runs and grows. It invades and occupies. It overflows [...].*[90]

We have to accept that fairies are already in our heads and parasites in our bodies, as one of the human protagonists is telling us at the end of *Phase IV*: 'We knew then we were being changed and made part of their world. We didn't know for what purpose. But we knew we would be told'. The next phase is: join the dance, in short: experiment.

Petra Lange-Berndt

Notes

1. Ward Muid, 'Beautifying Bones: A New Art and Its Inventor', *The Girl's Realm* (Bousefield Annual for 1903): 231–234, here 231.

2. Ibid., 234.

3. Lucy Lippard: 'Making Something from Nothing (Toward a Definition of Women's "Hobby Art")', *Heresies*, 1:4 (Heresis Collective, Winter 1978): 62–65; Petra Lange Berndt, *Animal Art. Präparierte Tierkörper in der Kunst, 1850–2000* (Munich: Verlag Silke Schreiber, 2009).

4. See exh.-cat. *Little Savages: Tessa Farmer* (London: Parabola and the Natural History Museum, 2007–2008).

5. See Marina Warner, *No Go the Bogeyman: Scaring, Lulling, and Making Mock* (London: Chatto and Windus, 1998), 173.

6. See Nicky Coutts, 'Portraits of the Nonhuman. Visualizations of the Malevolent Insect', in *Insect Poetics*, edited by Eric C. Brown (Minneapolis, London: University of Minnesota Press, 2006), 298–318, here 306.

7. Muid (1903), 231.

8. Tessa Farmer, *Touch Wood* (King's Wood, Kent. Stour Valley Arts, 2002).

9. Mannheim et al., *Duden Deutsches Universalwörterbuch*, 3rd printing (Bibliographisches Institut, 1996), 1367.

10. See Brian Massumi, 'Translator's Foreword: Pleasures of Philosophy' in Gilles Deleuze and Félix Guattari, *A Thousand Plateaus. Capitalism and Schizophrenia* (1980) (London and New York: University of Minnesota Press, 2009), ix–xvi, here xvf.

11. In Robert Hooke's journal *Micrographia; or, Some Physiological Descriptions of Minute Bodies Made by Magnifying Glasses, with Observations and Inquiries There Upon* (London 1665), the blown-up body of a flea is the most famous example.

12. Susan Stewart, *On Longing. Narratives of the Miniature, the Gigantic, the Souvenir, the Collection* (Durham, London: Duke University Press, 1993), 38.

13. Ibid., 54.

14. See Petra Lange-Berndt, 'Entrapped in Fairyland', in exh.-cat. *A World of Wild Doubt* (Berlin: Sternberg Press and Hamburger Kunstverein, 2013), 144–145.

15. Maurice Maeterlinck, *The Life of the Bee* (1901) (London: George Allen and Unwin, 1908), 220; see Niels Werber, *Ameisengesellschaften. Eine Faszinationsgeschichte* (Frankfurt am Main: S. Fischer Verlag, 2013), 140, for Maeterlinck's poetic method of research.

16. Deleuze and Guattari (1980/2009), 261, 265.

17. Farmer is not killing the insects used on purpose but collects them in the field, receives them as gifts or orders them via the internet.

18. Stewart (1993), 56.

19. See Charlotte Sleigh, 'Inside Out: The Unsettling Nature of Insects', in Brown (2006), 281–297, here 281.

20. Elias Canetti, *Crowds and Power* (1960) (New York: Gollancz, 1962), as quoted in Hugh Raffles, *Insectopedia* (New York: Pantheon Books, 2010), 121.

21. Deleuze and Guattari (1980/2009), 340.

22. Mark Dion as quoted in Justin Hoffmann, 'The Great Munich Bug Hunt. Ein Gespräch mit Mark Dion', *Kunst-Bulletin*, 3 (Hallwag, March 1994): 10–17, here 11f.

23. It is not a coincidence that surveys on the insect in art can be found in obscure literature such as Dipl.-Ing. Dr. Dr. h.c. Erwin Schimitschek, *Insekten in der Bildenden Kunst im Wandel der Zeiten in psychogenetischer Sicht* (Vienna: Naturhistorisches Museum, 1977).

24. We humans have learned from this strategy, see Jeffrey A. Lockwood, *Six-Legged Soldiers: Using Insects as Weapons of War* (Oxford and New York: Oxford University Press, 2009).

25. Coutts (2006), 301.

26. Maurice Maeterlinck, *The Life of the White Ant* (1927), 5th edition (London: George Allen and Unwin, 1944), 78f.

27. Ibid., 82. See also Charlotte Sleigh, *Six Legs Better. A Cultural History of Myrmecology* (Baltimore: John Hopkins University Press, 2007), 14f. for a discussion of the rhetorics that drive the metaphors and narrations of entomology.

28. Maeterlinck, *Bee* (1901/1908), 45.

29. Charles Darwin, *The Origin of Species* (1859) (London: Penguin Classics, 1985), 125.

30. Eugène N. Marais, *The Soul of the White Ant* (1925) (London: Jonathan Cape and Anthony Blond, 1971), 65.

31. See Adrian Eckersley, 'A Theme in the Early Work of Arthur Machen: "Degeneration"', *Literature in Transition*, 35: 3 (January 1992): 277–287, here 285.

32. Arthur Machen, *The Three Impostors* (1895) (London: Dover Publications Inc., 2007). Other relevant stories are 'The Red Hand' (1895), 'The Shining Pyramid' (1895), 'The White People' (1906), 'Out of the Earth' (1915).

33. Arthur Machen, 'Folklore and Legends of the North', *Literature* (24 September 1898): 272, as quoted in *The Line of Terror and Other Essays*, edited by S. T. Joshi (Bristol: Hobgoblin Press, 1997), 31.

34. Machen (1895/2007), 61; see also Sage Leslie-McCarthy: 'Re-Vitalising the Little People: Arthur Machen's Tales of the Remnant Races', *Australasian Victorian Studies Journal*, 11 (2005): 65–78, here 66.

35. Machen (1895/2007), 82.

36. Eckersley (1992), 282.

37. Machen (1985/2007), 66; see also Katharine Briggs, *An Encyclopaedia of Fairies: Hobgoblins, Brownies, Bogies, and Other Supernatural Creatures* (New York: Pantheon

Books, 1976), 21, 419.

38. Carole G. Silver, *Strange and Secret Peoples: Fairies and Victorian Consciousness* (Oxford and New York: Oxford University Press, 1999), 150.

39. Deleuze and Guattari (1980/2009), 286.

40. Mary Douglas, *Purity and Danger. An Analysis of Concepts of Pollution and Taboo* (1966) (*Collected Works*, vol. II) (London and New York: Routledge, 2003), 103.

41. Deleuze and Guattari (1980/2009), 274.

42. Carl Linné as quoted in Paul Armand Gette: 'Introduction', in Ibid. and Bernard Durin: *Insects Etc. An Anthology of Arthropods Featuring a Bounty of Beetles* (1980) (New York: Hudson Hills Press Inc., 1981), 7–21, here 7.

43. For a debate of the swarm as collective without centre from the perspective of media studies, see Eva Horn and Lucas Marco Gisi (eds.), *Schwärme — Kollektive ohne Zentrum. Eine Wissensgeschichte zwischen Leben und Information* (Bielefeld: Transcript, 2009).

44. Sleigh (2006), 294; Bert Hölldobler and Edward O. Wilson, *The Superorganism. The Beauty, Elegance, and Strangeness of Insect Societies* (New York and London: W. W. Norton and Company, Inc., 2009), 178. Especially in the case of ants one can detect an alternating interest in models, methods and discourses within entomology, economic theories, sociology, and anthropology since the late nineteenth century, see Werber (2013), 24 ff.

45. Peter Kropotkin, *Mutual Aid: A Factor of Evolution* (1902) (London: Freedom Press, 1987), 17–33, 135f.; Raffles (2010), 66.

46. Claire Preston, *Bee* (London: Reaktion Books, 2006), 15; see also Jacques Derrida, '"Fourmis", Hélène Cixous and Mireille Calle-Gruber, Lectures de la Différence Sexuelle', in *Hélène Cixous: Rootprints. Memory and Live Writing*, edited by Hélène Cixous and Mireille Calle-Gruber (London and New York: Routledge, 1997), 119–127.

47. Hölldobler and Wilson (2009), XVII. For a critique, especially of Wilson, see Charlotte Sleigh, *Ant* (London: Reaktion Books, 2003), 169 ff.

48. Marais (1925/1971), 15, 30.

49. Hölldobler and Wilson (2009), 118, 408.

50. Ibid., 408; Maeterlink (1927/1944), 77.

51. Sleigh (2003), 28 ff., 69 ff.

52. Maeterlink (1901/1908), 130.

53. Ibid., 190; Hölldobler and Wilson (2009), 417.

54. Marais (1925/1971), 110.

55. William Morton Wheeler, 'The Ant-Colony as an Organism', *The Journal of Morphology*, 22:2 (1911): 307–325, here 310; see also Marais (1925/1971), 5. This sensibility did not prevent Wheeler from speculations around eugenics, see Werber (2013), 47.

56. Marais (1925/1971), 50 ff.

57. Hölldobler and Wilson (2009), 85; Deleuze and Guattari (1980/2009), 165.

58. See exh.-cat. *Swarm* (Philadelphia: The Fabric Workshop and Museum, 2005); Sebastian Vehlken: 'Zootechnologies: Swarming as a Cultural Technique', *Theory, Culture & Society* (published online 10 June 2013): http://tcs.sagepub.com/content/early/2013/06/09/0263276413488959, 1–22, here 2.

59. See exh.-cat. *Alastair Mackie — Corpse* (London: All Visual Arts, 2011), 32 ff.

60. Kurt Ranke and Josef R. Klíma, 'Biene', in *Enzyklopädie des Märchens*, 2 (Berlin and New York: De Gruyter, 1977), 296–307, here 301f.

61. Sleigh (2003), 87ff.; Preston (2006), 122, 149.

62. Petra Lange-Berndt, 'Vom Bienenschwarm zum Mottenlicht. Insekten im Spiel- und Experimentalfilm', in *Tiere im Film — eine Menschheitsgeschichte der Moderne*, edited by Maren Möhring, Massimo Perinelli, Olaf Stieglitz (Cologne, Weimar and Vienna: Böhlau, 2009), 207–219, here 211 ff.

63. Raffles (2010), 7, 11.

64. Deleuze and Guattari (1980/2009), 240.

65. Sleigh (2006), 283f.

66. Sigmund Freud, 'Notiz über den "Wunderblock"' (1925) in *Sigmund Freud Studienausgabe III: Psychologie des Unbewußten* (Frankfurt am Main: Fischer Taschenbuch Verlag, 2000), 363–369.

67. Deleuze and Guattari (1980/2009), 10, 271.

68. Maeterlinck (1901/1908), 65; see for a discussion of plasticity in relation to modern and contemporary art Dietmar Rübel, *Plastizität. Eine Kunstgeschichte des Veränderlichen* (Munich: Silke Schreiber Verlag, 2012).

69. Jacques Derrida, *Archive Fever* (1995) (Chicago and London: University of Chicago Press, 1998).

70. Maeterlinck (1901/1908), 249, 252, 263.

71. Deleuze and Guattari (1980/2009), 266.

72. Gavin R. Broad, 'Anonymous Doors', in *Little Savages* (2007–2008), 10–13, here 11.

73. Tessa Farmer, 'The Fairies Are Coming', press release (London: Viktor Wynd Fine Art, 2011).

74. Michel Serres, *The Parasite* (1980) (Minneapolis and London: University of Minnesota Press, 2007), 217.

75. Ibid., 3.

76. Ibid., 36.

77. Ibid., 196.

78. Ibid., 190–191. As Werber (2013), 337, points out, in parallel to Michel Serres and Saul Bass, biologist and palaeontologist, Lynn Margulis, has been advocating an alternative theory of evolution: not only mutation enables variation, but as a rule

variation is happening through incorporation: all organisms are permeated by parasites and symbionts who are continuously exchanging their RNA with their hosts regardless of possible consequences.

79. Serres (1980/2007), 78, 167.

80. Vehlken (2013), 3, 13.

81. Viktor Wynd press release (2011).

82. Deleuze and Guattari (1980/2009), 269; see for Bass Werber (2013), 335 ff.

83. See exh.-cat. *Animal Art* (Steirischer Herbst, Galerie Hanns Christian Hoschek, Graz 1987); Liz Brooks, 'The Spirit of the Hive, Mark Thompson's Invocations', *Performance* (London), 62 (November 1990): 8–15, here 11; Petra Lange-Berndt "'Das Zeitalter der Insekten" Künstlerische Partnerschaften mit Ameisen und Bienen', in *Ich, das Tier. Tiere als Persönlichkeiten in der Kulturgeschichte*, edited by Heike Fuhlbrügge, Jessica Ullrich, Friedrich Weltzien (Berlin: Dietrich Reimer Verlag, 2008), 133 143.

84. Interview with the artist (24 February 2007).

85. See for the cultural history of the male beekeeper Siegfried Becker, 'Der Bienenvater. Zur kulturellen Stilisierung der Imkerei in der Industriegesellschaft,' *Hessische Blätter für Volks- und Kulturforschung*, Neue Folge, 27 (1991): 163–194.

86. Tessa Farmer as quoted in 'Arthur in the Underworld,' *BBC Radio* 4 (4 July 2013), 30 min.

87. Serres (1980/2007), 72, 133, 144.

88. Donna Haraway, *Primate Visions Gender, Race, and Nature In the World of Modern Science* (New York and London: Routledge, 1989).

89. Maeterlinck (1927/1944), 117.

90. Serres (1980/2007), 253.

Horrifically Delightful
Giovanni Aloi

As an intellectual figure involved in the twentieth century surrealist movement, Georges Bataille's (1897–1962) visions of an alternative cosmos proposed a unique departure from the mischievousness of dada's cultural debris and amply surpassed the twisted imaginations of his colleagues. In his absurdly shocking reconfiguring of the world, he was able to summon a sense of tangible urgency, a seductively horrific plausibility oscillating between the tempting impossibility of re-inventing scientific anthropology and the tantalising call for the devising of a mythological anthropology.

In his proposal for an alternative perception of the cosmos, Bataille unravelled a then unparalleled visionary realm in which extreme seductiveness was at the boundary of horror.[1] So began 'Eye' (1929), a very short text in which Bataille acknowledged the irresistible fascination that draws man to look closer in and deeper, not in order to find truth and beauty but to come into uncomfortable closeness with the horrifically delightful. To best outline his original thesis, Bataille turned to insects, claiming that '[t]he fear of insects is no doubt one of the most singular and most developed of these horrors...'[2] an extremely seductive horror which he linked to the 'fear of the eye'.[3] A fear triggered by the ambivalent opportunity for horror and beauty hidden by the utter inexpressiveness of the organ itself. It is a common misconception in our everyday lives to think of the eye not as the bulbus oculi, the spherical body constituted by the optical nerves, sclera, iris and pupil, but as the organ framed by the eye lids, eyebrows and surrounding facial areas. On the basis of this gross generalisation, we attribute the human eye with superior expressive abilities that somehow surpass the eyes of other mammals and other groups of animals. If extracted from the orb, however, the eye of a human will cease to be a 'window onto the soul' and become as devoid of expression as that of a cow, a pig or a bird. Extrapolated from the orb, and consequently from the facial fleshiness which conveys expressiveness to the eye, all eyes, both human and animal are, therefore, equally inexpressive.

The case of insects is a special one, one in which the seductive horror of the fear of the eye, the fear of the inexpressiveness of the organ itself and its unwillingness to reveal the intentions of the other, is exacerbated by the absolute lack of facial fleshiness. The chitinous segmentations of insect faces present the eye, as in fish and reptiles, for what it is: an utterly inexpressive organ, like all others constituting the body, but one upon which our anthropomorphic expectations of expressiveness have been bestowed for millennia. Phrases such as 'I see fear in your eyes' or '...a twinkle in her eyes' are grounded on commonplace generalisations attributing substantial expressiveness to the organ-eye and transforming it therefore in the eye of the conscience, an organ even exceeding expressiveness for the purpose of absorbing the spectacle, scrutinising it and ultimately, judging it.[4]

Lacking the fleshiness of the face required to express, insects, crustaceans, fish, amphibians and reptiles all fall into a category of conscience-less beings — Levinas' animal without a face[5], the Cartesian automata.[6] It is this Cartesian rationality that Bataille aimed to subvert through the re-imagining of the very small gland called the pineal eye, which resides as a vestigial eye, at the centre of our brain. Descartes regarded it as the principal situ of the soul, the mediator between the external visions provided by the eyes and the reasoning of such visions as computed by the rest of the brain. He knew that animals also have pineal glands but denied them the importance that the organ plays in humans as, according to him, animals did not have souls.[7] Bataille's conception of the pineal eye is instead that of an organ through which a devaluation of conventional visuality can be operated for the purpose of envisioning an alternative cosmos oscillating between extreme seductiveness and the boundary of horror. Conventional visuality, that which the eyes enable us to see, is therefore implicitly subjugated by the rationalising ordering systems of the mind, whilst the pineal eye represents an opportunity for radically reconfiguring visuality, our relationship to the outside world, and triggering a re-understanding of the cosmos. Escaping conventional visuality or in other words, abandoning any cultural certainties for the purpose of reconfiguring a new visceral and pulsating cosmos, may not necessarily lead to beauty or truth. It certainly does not in Bataille's case, but, as I will argue, it may enable us to find the courage to look beyond the appearances of what we have been told to see and believe, providing a valuable opportunity to reclaim the cosmos at least in the sphere of the personal experience.

Tessa Farmer's work vastly relies on a shift involving conventional visual experience and the visionary, mythological representations proposed by the pineal eye. I remember the first time I encountered a piece by Farmer in a small gallery in London's East End. Upon entering the exhibition space I was confronted by a number of works of art in different media, some more traditional than others, but I was not quite prepared for the phenomenology her work sets up. I had heard quite a bit about Farmer's work before, but I had not seen any images of it yet.

In one corner of the gallery, hovering twenty or thirty centimetres from the ground, was a small dotting of lightly-swaying insect-like bodies. From about three feet away, it looked like some flies and a few wasps had curiously gathered together in a corner of the gallery. The threads suspending them from the ceiling were entirely invisible in the specially-darkened exhibiting space. Like other works of art on a miniature scale, Farmer's work invites the viewer to get closer and closer, something which challenges the certainties of vision, that requires re-focussing on the elusive image and reconsidering what is being really seen. As I leant closer, what initially appeared to be flies, revealed themselves as something rather different. With some amount of astonishment, I had to concede that I was indeed looking at very minute skeletons with insect wings. Their tiny skulls, fragile rib cages, and thin legs and arms looked too accurately detailed not to be perceived as real entomological beings. The more I looked, the more the attempt to rationally make sense of the scene failed to resolve. Not only did the minute skeletons look too real to be untrue, but they also seemed to be doing pretty nasty things to the insects in their proximity. Wrestling some of them, armed with hedgehog spikes as spears and riding dragonflies like unwelcome hitch-hikers on an 'insect-flyway', these little creatures were uniformly blending with what a century of scientific research had carefully classified in the taxonomy of natural history. What is one to make of such vision? What would science say about this overwhelming piece of evidence? Is this the final proof that fairies exist? And why is one seduced into looking more and more whilst the horrific little scene unravels upon one's incredulous eye?

Although mesmerising, the utter plausibility of Farmer's fairies is conferred by a number of credible factors. Her painstakingly crafted fairies match the infinitesimal scale and detailed intricacy of similarly-sized insects such as flies, wasps or bees. In the attempt to rationalise the scene, conventional visuality leads to the perception of likeness between what is truly natural (and once was alive) and what isn't, inextricably confounding the two in a baffling, illusionary game.

What we are presented with, I would suggest, is a surrealist vision in which the inexpressive eyes of insects hide any decipherable feeling, just as the hollow orbs of the fairies deny access to their real thoughts and intentions. Here, insects and fairies are equally unsettling in their silent, ambiguous being. The enigmatic *trompe l'oeil* seduces its viewer not only to look longer, harder and deeper, but simultaneously demands a suspension of disbelief stronger than that incited by film and literature, for what we are presented with is not mediated by celluloid or printed paper but three-dimensional beings positioned right in front of our very eyes. How far can we go in suspending our disbelief is the question, and how horrific would this beauty feel if we should abandon ourselves to this vision?

Farmer's work clearly echoes the Victorian fascination for fairies and the obsession with the new cultures of visuality which at the time were enthusing large audiences. The proliferation of photographic images and the wider and cheaper distribution of them caused a dramatic change in visual consumption. According to Lorraine Daston and Peter Galison, authors of *Objectivity* (2007), the view of the world seen through the lenses of the camera and printed onto photographic paper, gave rise to the challenge of producing 'ethical-epistemic mechanical objectivity'.[8] By mechanical objectivity Daston and Galison expressly connote the will to repress the intervention and interpretation of the artist-author, and to operate a 'set of procedures that would, as it were, move nature to the page through a strict protocol, if not automatically'.[9] The authors acknowledge that this constituted a form of utopianism; minimisation of intervention and interpretation was all that could effectively be achieved, as a process of idealisation was unavoidable. This is but one aspect which Farmer's work accomplishes: the apparent removal of the artist in the attempt to provide a seamless cohesion between natural and man-made. In her work, the result is overwhelming, so much so that it strikes the more savvy viewers of today as reliving the 'seeing is believing' credulity experienced by Victorian audiences.

By the 1860s, through the publication of natural history atlases, the newly-disciplined, scientific, highly-restrained way of 'scientific-seeing' was already widespread, propelling the concept of scientific objectivity as the main lens through which to look at the world.[10] The cultural impact resulting from this experience on the nineteenth century city dwellers of Paris and London (the Natural History Museum opened there in 1883) was significant, and triggered a pronounced amateurial frenzy for non-institutional practices such as witnessing, collecting, cataloguing, beach-combing, geology, gazing at exotic animals and collecting ferns, which still makes the Victorian era unique in its eccentric thirst for knowledge.[11] The accessibility granted to the nature optic had repercussions on the Victorian optic in ways that also influenced the arts. A reliance on observation rather than on theory was, in fact, one of the things that set natural history apart from much of the science practiced in universities. The aesthetic of particularity that we have become accustomed to in examining the work of John Ruskin, the Pre-Raphaelites, and Gerard Manley Hopkins was trained through the Victorian fascination with scrutinising nature. It was a legacy from romanticism funnelled through the lens of Victorian natural historians, who looked with the naked eye, the hand lens, the microscope, and the telescope until they had their fill.[12]

It is this sense of excitement for discovery through the eye, the possibility of charting the un-mapped of the natural onto the supernatural nurtured through the Victorian age, that Farmer's work magically reignites. However, Farmer's installations should not be simply understood as a nostalgia project, something akin to the revival of vinyl records, taxidermy and retro-photography that we have witnessed over the past ten years in the arts and crafts. There is something more interesting in her proposal to re-envisage a new, alternative cosmos, today.

Like photographic evidence in the nineteenth century, Farmer's use of real, preserved insects and crustaceans carries an indexical reference advancing claims of truth: the natural surface of the animals. The encounter with preserved entomological specimens traditionally has become an experience confined to the collections of natural history museums. Within that setting, the display of specimens is invested with epistemological value. The specimens are displayed in the cabinets as representatives of a multitude of other living (or extinct) insects around the world. The schemata for this reading are given to us by the longstanding tradition of taxonomy which began in the late seventeenth century. It is an understanding of insects entirely orchestrated by scientific rigor, the rigor of visibility which enables comparison. The insects we encounter in Farmer's installations are very much the same although they are more regularly less pristine than their museum counterparts. This is because Farmer's insects do not inhabit the same timeless space in which museum specimens exist; hers are caught in the moment of a complex, dynamic narrative that has nothing to do with Darwinian evolution and taxonomy. To become caught up in Farmer's tableaux means, returning to Bataille to abandon the epistemological supremacy which vision gained during the classical age of science, the Enlightenment, for the purpose of allowing the emergence of a mythological anthropology in the place of a scientific one.

In today's Western culture, we seem to have implicitly accepted the scientific lens as the one and only viable filter through which perception of the natural world can take place. Pressed by the catastrophic prophecies of global warming and mass extinction, what we are left with is a hollow natural world made of figures and statistics. Nature is a value to stabilise and preserve rather than something we are free to really connect with in a creative and interiorised way. Nature is something to market, sell and purchase, but it can no longer play a poetic, mythological role. What would be the challenges involved in re-thinking our relationship to animals and plants beyond the visibilities enabled by the scientific lens? How would our relationship to nature change if we stopped to reduce it to a resource or something that we have to preserve for our children? What if animals and plants could still, as in Greek mythology, become believably entangled in complex and enchanting narratives in which they become more than a Latin binomial? What if we enabled a less rationalised, pragmatic vision of nature to emerge? Would we then find reasons to understand things differently and prevent the catastrophic vision which the future holds?

Bataille's proposal for a mythological anthropology not based on conventional visuality provided by the eyes, but on the pineal eye's ability to transcend pragmatism, begins with the reduction of 'science to a state that must be defined by the term subordination [...] for nothing could keep science from blindly emptying the universe of its human content'.[13] It is within this optic that Farmer's narratives, although relaying on the indexical veridicity purported by the surfaces of her specimens, exceed the natural history diorama by imbuing nature with a newly-found mythological charge. In one of her tableaux, entitled

The Perilous Pursuit of a Python (2013; Fig 11: see colour insert), crabs, ants, spiders and bees all co-operate in the attack on a threatening python. Rather worryingly, her narratives unravel in a world where human beings are entirely absent — this too is simultaneously horrific and beautifully enchanting. Perhaps the artist exposes a perception of nature that is as believable as the scientific one, but that is simply inaccessible to us. Perhaps, that's what animals do when we turn away. Ultimately, the absence of humans in Farmer's tableaux renders her scenes a-temporal. They can be equally understood as referring to a remote past in which humans had not yet arrived, in which perhaps they were preceded by fairies, or to a future in which we no longer exist and fairies are attempting to fill our place in the subjugation of a rebelling natural world.

Notes

1. Georges Bataille, 'Eye', *Visions of Excess: Selected Writings 1927–1939*, edited by A. Stoekl (Minnesota University Press, 1985).
2. Ibid., 17.
3. Ibid.
4. Ibid., 19.
5. In Levinas' phenomenological discussion, otherness occupies a kind of primacy which in realm of the encounter is always unknowable. The Face becomes the threshold through which ethical obligation is established amongst beings and the unknowability of the other is the one element which continuously calls for a furthering of the relational. A totalisation occurs when limits are placed on the other, when the other is, so to speak, pre-emptied of its unknowability, repressing a denial of difference and autonomy. Levinas' consideration of the animal as other becomes further problematised by his distinction between mammals and non-mammals through the apparent biological condition by which 'lower' animals are culturally segregated. In *The Provocation of Levinas: Rethinking the Other* (1988), Levinas was asked to elucidate his 'ethics of alterity' on the non-human. Then he stated that the animal face is merely 'biological' and that as a result it does not command an ethical response. 'I cannot say at what moment you have the right to be called face. The human face is completely different and only afterwards we discover the face of an animal. I don't know if a snake has a face...' (1988 :168–80)

6. In 1641, Descartes theorised a mechanised vision of the universe in which animals are nothing more than automata without a soul. This vision has greatly influenced our relationship with animals ever since.

7. Descartes' interest in the pineal gland was expressed in a number of works. The first mention of the pineal gland can be found in his *Treatise of Man* posthumously published in 1662 and more prominently in his 1649 *The Passions of The Soul*.

8. Lorraine Daston and Peter Galison, *Objectivity* (New York, Zone Books, 2007), 121

9. Ibid., 121.

10. Ibid., 122.

11. B.T. Gates, 'Introduction: Why Victorian Natural History?' *Victorian Literature and Culture*, 35:1 (September, 2007), 539.

12. Ibid., 540.

13. Bataille, 'Eye', 80–81.

Colour images

1. Tessa Farmer, *Cosmic Cloud*, 2012. Bones, insects, plant roots, metal, glass, gold and aluminium leaf, electronic components, exhibition *Flights of Fancy*, Tatton Park Biennial, Knutsford, UK 2012. Photo credit Thierry Bal. Reproduced with kind permission of the artist.

2. Mat Collishaw, *Butterflies and Flowers*, 2005. Dura Transparency, Lightbox © Mat Collishaw. All Rights Reserved, DACS 2015.

3. Joseph Cornell, *Untitled (Butterfly Habitat)*, c.1940. Box construction with painted glass. 12 x 9 1/8 x 3 1/8 in. Lindy and Edwin Bergman Joseph Cornell Collection, 1982.1845, The Art Institute of Chicago © The Joseph and Robert Cornell Memorial Foundation/VAGA, NY/DACS, London 2015.

4. Sir Joseph Noel Paton, *The Reconciliation of Oberon and Titania*, 1847. Oil on canvas. Image courtesy of Scottish National Gallery.

5. Richard Dadd, *The Fairy Feller's Master-Stroke*, 1855–64. Oil on canvas. © Tate, London 2015.

6. Tessa Farmer, *The Horde (detail)*. Insects, spiders, lizards, seahorses, mouse and rat bones, porcupine quills, hedgehog quills, sea urchin spines, plant roots, glue, lighting, installation at the Hamburger Kunstverein/exhibition *A World of Wild Doubt*, 2013. Photo credit Olaf Pascheit.

7. Tessa Farmer, *A Prize Catch*, 2010. Desiccated blue tit, insects, plant roots, hedgehog spines. Photo credit Galerie Antje Wachs, Berlin.

8. Tessa Farmer, *The Coming of The Fairies (detail)*, 2011. Taxidermy swan, insects, plant roots. Photo credit Tessa Farmer.

9. Richard Doyle, *Fairy Rings and Toadstools*, watercolour and gouache, 1875, Leicester Galleries.

10. Arthur Rackham, *The Kensington Gardens Are in London Where the King Lives*, lithograph from J.M. Barrie, *Peter Pan in Kensington Gardens*, London 1906.

11. Tessa Farmer, *The Perilous Pursuit of a Python*, 2013. Insects, crustaceans, taxidermied snake, bones, plant roots, temporary installation at New Art Gallery Walsall, exhibition *The Nature of the Beast*. Photo credit New Art Gallery Walsall.

12. Tessa Farmer, *The Depraved Pursuit of a Possum*, 2013. Commissioned for *Red Queen* at MONA, Tasmania. Insects, arachnids, plant roots, wasp nest, crab claws, crabs, sponge, banksia pod, bones, shark egg case, freeze dried brush tailed possum. Most of the materials were collected in Tasmania. Photo credit Tessa Farmer.

13. Film still from *Phase IV*, feature film, directed by Saul Bass, USA, 1974.

14. Film still from *Phase IV*, feature film, directed by Saul Bass, USA, 1974.

Colour images

Black and white images

Contributors

Giovanni Aloi is Lecturer in Art History, Theory and Criticism in the School of the Art Institute of Chicago. In 2006, he founded *Antennae, the Journal of Nature in Visual Culture* of which he is currently Editor in Chief (www.antennae.org.uk).

Gail-Nina Anderson is an art historian based in Newcastle upon Tyne. She obtained her PhD from Nottingham University for a thesis on the iconography of Dante Gabriel Rossetti's later paintings.

Gavin R. Broad is Curator of Hymenoptera at the Natural History Museum. Since 2006, Gavin's research interests are focused on the taxonomy and diversity of parasitoid wasps of the family *Ichneumonidae*.

Brian Catling is a poet and performance artist. He is Professor of Fine Art at The Ruskin School of Drawing and Fine Art, Oxford.

Jeremy Harte is a researcher into folklore and archaeology, with a particular interest in sacred space and tales of encounters with the supernatural. His book *Explore Fairy Traditions* won the Katharine Briggs award of the Folklore Society for 2005.

Catriona McAra is Curatorial and Exhibitions Manager at Leeds College of Art. Since 2011, she has published widely on Farmer's work. McAra is interested in artistic engagement with the sciences, and the fairy tale in contemporary creative practice.

Petra Lange-Berndt is Chair for Modern and Contemporary Art, Kunstgeschichtliches Seminar, University of Hamburg, as well as a curator. She has published the book *Animal Art: Präparierte Tiere in der Kunst 1850–2000* (Munich: Silke Schreiber, 2009).

John Sears is the author of *Reading George Szirtes* (2008) and *Stephen King's Gothic* (2011). With Patricia Allmer he co-curated *Taking Shots: The Photography of William S. Burroughs* at The Photographers' Gallery in London (2014).

Acknowledgements
The editor would like to thank the contributors and the following people: Danielle Arnaud; Richard Bancroft; Kate Bernheimer; Niall and Soren Campbell; Marion Endt-Jones; Marjorie Lloyd; Marianne McAra; Mark Pilkington; Tihana Šare; Viktor Wynd. This book is dedicated to Tessa and the fairies for many years of friendship and fascination.

The artist would like to thank Petra Lange Berndt, Gavin R. Broad, Jeremy Harte, Gail-Nina Anderson, Brian Catling, Giovanni Aloi, John Sears, Mark Pilkington, Jamie Sutcliffe, Tihana Sare and Catriona McAra for her unwavering support over the years and dedication to this book.

About Tessa Farmer

1978   Born in Birmingham, England

EDUCATION

2002–2003   MFA in Fine Art, Ruskin School of Drawing and Fine Art, University of Oxford

1997–2000   BFA (Hons) in Fine Art (First Class), Ruskin School of Drawing and Fine Art, University of Oxford

SELECTED SOLO EXHIBITIONS

2015   *In Fairyland*, Viktor Wynd Museum of Curiosities, Natural History and Fine Art, London

2015   *In Fairyland*, Leeds College of Art (with Annelies Strba, Sverre Mälling, Su Blackwell and the Cottingley Fairies)

2014   *Unwelcome Visitors*, The Holburne Museum, Bath

2012   *ISAM:Control Over Nature*, collaboration with Amon Tobin, Spencer Brownstone Gallery, New York

2012   *From The Deep*, Millennium, St Ives

2011   *The Coming of The Fairies*, Viktor Wynd Fine Art, London

2011   *ISAM: Control Over Nature*, collaboration with Amon Tobin, Crypt Gallery, London

2011   *Nymphidia*, Danielle Arnaud Contemporary Art, London

2008   Spencer Brownstone Gallery, New York

2007   *Little Savages*, Natural History Museum, London

         Infestation, Chapter Arts Centre, Cardiff

2006   *The Terror*, Firstsite, Colchester

2002   *Touch Wood*, Rochester Art Gallery, Rochester

SELECTED GROUP EXHIBITIONS

2016   *Sneakyville*, Haugar Vestfold Kunstmuseum, Norway

         Pastoral Noir, Wood Street Galleries, Pittsburgh

         Perfectionism III, Griffin Gallery, London

         Strange Worlds: The Vision of Angela Carter, Royal West of England Academy, Bristol

2015   *Step in Stone*, Somerset

         The Gallery of Wonder on Tour, Northumberland

         Unnatural Curiosities, Viktor Wynd Museum of Curiosities, London

2014 *The Infected Museum*, Viktor Wynd Museum of Curiosities, London

      Secret Lives, Beaux Arts, Bath

      Odyssey, St Edmund the King Church, London

      Apiculture: Bees and the Art of Pollination, Peninsula Art Gallery, Plymouth

2013 *Victoriana*, Guildhall Art Gallery, London

      World Fantasy Convention, Brighton

      Beautiful Minds, Kleine Galerie, Humboldt University, Berlin

      Red Queen, MONA, Tasmania

      The Nature of the Beast, New Art Gallery Walsall

      Odyssey, Bath Abbey, Bath

      From Grimm to Reality, Sidney Cooper Gallery, Canterbury

      Beastly Hall, Bexley Hall, Kent

      Oscillator, Science Gallery, Dublin

      World of Wild Doubt, Hamburg Kunstverein, Germany

2012 *Bedlam* , Old Vic Tunnels, London. Organised by Lazarides Gallery, London

      Pertaining to Things Natural, Chelsea Physic Garden and John Martin Gallery, London

      Tatton Park Biennial, Tatton Park, Knutsford

      Minimal, Hå Gamle Prestegard, Norway

      Hunters and Hunted, Museum Villa Rot, Germany

2011 *Saatchi Gallery in Adelaide, British Art Now*, Art Gallery of South Australia

      Lafcadio's Revenge (with Dana Sherwood and Nina Nichols), New Orleans, USA

      Mindful, The Old Vic Tunnels, London

      Inaugural exhibition, Museum of Old and New Art (MONA), Tasmania Australia

      The Charter of The Forest, The Collection, Lincoln Art Gallery

      House of Beasts, Attingham Park (National Trust), Shrewsbury

      Enchanted Garden, Flower Fairies and Dark Tales, Mottisfont Abbey (National Trust) Hampshire

2010 *Cabinet*, John Martin Gallery, London

      The Witching Hour, Birmingham Museum and Art Gallery (Water Hall), Birmingham

      Newspeak: British Art Now: Part Two, Saatchi Gallery, London

      Provenance (Exhibition and Symposium), Corsham Court, Bath

      Revelation Film Festival (screening of An Insidious Intrusion and Nest of the Skeletons), Perth, Australia

      Fairytales: The Surreal House, Barbican, London: 10th June- evening screening of An Insidious Intrusion.

Larger than Life Stranger than Fiction, Eleventh Triennial of Small Scale Sculpture, Fellbach, Germany

Oasis, Bury St Edmunds Art Gallery, Bury St Edmunds

Dead or Alive, Museum of Arts and Design, New York

Extraordinary Measures, Belsay Hall, Northumberland

East Wing IX: Exhibitionism, The Courtauld Institute, London

2009 *Newspeak, British Art Now*, The State Hermitage Museum, St Petersburg, Russia

Pestival, South Bank Centre, London

Slump City, Space Studios, London

2008 *Riddle Me*, Danielle Arnaud Gallery, London, UK

Wrap Your Troubles in a Dream, curated by Power Ekroth, Lautom Gallery, Oslo, Norway

In Transit, Ladbroke Grove, London

Animal Magic, Eleven, London, UK

Tatton Park Biennial, Knutsford, UK

LOCKED IN:The Visible, Casino Luxembourg, Luxembourg

Gothic, Fieldgate Gallery, London

2007 *The Future Can Wait*, Atlantis Gallery, London, UK

Growing Wild, Andreiana Mihail Gallery, curated by Jane Neal, Bucharest, Romania

Am Schlimmsten: nicht im Sommer sterben, Nassauische Kunstverein, Wiesbaden, Germany

2006 *Repatriating the Ark*, Museum of Garden History, London

Miniature Worlds, Jerwood Space, London

Where the Wild Things Are, Imperial College, London

2005 *The Unlimited Dream Company*, The Biscuit Factory, Newcastle

Thinking the Unthinkable, Northern Gallery for Contemporary Art, Sunderland

New Sculpture, Museum 52, London

The Young Ones, Said Business School, Oxford

2004 *Bloomberg New Contemporaries*, The Barbican, London

Bloomberg New Contemporaries, The Coach Shed, Liverpool

2002 *Tweede Natuur*, Lia Schelkens Sculpture Gallery, Antwerp

COLLECTIONS

Saatchi Collection, London · David Roberts Collection, London · Libeert Collection, Belgium Ashmolean Museum, Oxford · MONA (Museum of Old and New Art) Hobart, Australia 21 Century Museum, Kentucky, USA · George Hartman Collection, Toronto · Private collections in UK, Europe, Australia and USA